P9-CKV-905

Josh Was Still Trying to Tease Me, Teach Me, Rescue Me, Better Me . . . Which I Totally Hate!

Josh followed me into the den. "I hope you're not thinking of staying here," I said.

"Nope. I got a place in Westwood near school."

I flicked on the TV. He collapsed onto the couch. *Beavis and Butthead* was on. "Wouldn't it be better if you went to college back East?" I suggested. "They say girls at NYU aren't at all particular."

He grabbed the remote and switched to CNN.

"You know, in some parts of the universe—maybe not in Contempo Casuals—but in some parts, Cher, it's considered cool to know what's going on in the world."

It was déjà vu all over again. Josh had returned to better my life. I stuffed the remote down between the couch cushions, out of his reach. "Oh, thank you, Josh," I said. "I so need lessons from you on how to be cool. Tell me the part about Kenny G. again."

For orders other than by individual consumers, Pocket Books grants a discount on the purchase of **10 or more** copies of single titles for special markets or premium use. For further details, please write to the Vice-President of Special Markets, Pocket Books, 1230 Avenue of the Americas, New York, NY 10020.

For information on how individual consumers can place orders, please write to Mail Order Department, Paramount Publishing, 200 Old Tappan Road, Old Tappan, NJ 07675.

CLUELESS

A novel by H. B. Gilmour
Based on the film written and
directed by Amy Heckerling

AN ARCHWAY PAPERBACK
Published by POCKET BOOKS
New York   London   Toronto   Sydney   Tokyo   Singapore

The sale of this book without its cover is unauthorized. If you purchased this book without a cover, you should be aware that it was reported to the publisher as "unsold and destroyed." Neither the author nor the publisher has received payment for the sale of this "stripped book."

This book is a work of fiction. Names, characters, places and incidents are products of the author's imagination or are used fictitiously. Any resemblance to actual events or locales or persons, living or dead, is entirely coincidental.

AN ARCHWAY PAPERBACK *Original*

An Archway Paperback published by
POCKET BOOKS, a division of Simon & Schuster Inc.
1230 Avenue of the Americas, New York, NY 10020

TM and copyright © 1995 by Paramount Pictures

All rights reserved, including the right to reproduce
this book or portions thereof in any form whatsoever.
For information address Pocket Books, 1230 Avenue
of the Americas, New York, NY 10020

ISBN: 0-671-53631-1

First Archway Paperback printing August 1995

10 9 8 7 6 5 4 3 2 1

AN ARCHWAY PAPERBACK and colophon are
registered trademarks of Simon & Schuster Inc.

Printed in the U.S.A.

IL: 7+

For Anne, Amber, John, Wendy, and,
as always, Jess, with love

Chapter 1

I had this dream a couple of months back. It was about my mom. She died when I was just a baby. A fluke accident during a routine liposuction is what I tell people. My mom was a seriously stunning disco babe. A real Betty. There's a portrait of her in go-go boots hanging in our living room, which is about the size of the Coliseum but done in polished pink Italian marble and ankle-deep cream carpeting instead of AstroTurf.

Anyway, in this dream, I'm like catching her up on my life. I tell her about my best friend, Dionne, one of *the* major Bettys of Beverly Hills High. And how we ride around town with other cute kids in the cherry red Jeep my dad, the Litigator, gave me for my birthday. I paint her a picture of me and my pals striding through the high school halls, styled hair cleanly bouncing, makeup salon fresh, fat-free bodies aerobicized to sinewy perfection. We are the world, we are the in crowd.

I want my mom to rest assured. I want her to know I'm okay. So I don't say how much I miss her. I don't even mention my childhood fantasy of us shopping Rodeo Drive together in these adorable mother-daughter outfits with matching Visa Gold cards. No. I keep it light and breezy so she won't get bored. So she'll stick around.

"My life is so fun. It's like: Help! I'm trapped in a Noxzema commercial," I quip to her. I feel like I'll hurl if she leaves me again. So I let her know that basically I'm beautiful, rich, and happy.

Then I'm waiting for her to tell me how glad she is. Or proud. Whatever. Her hair's all poufed out in this total bouffant. It sways as she shakes her head sadly.

"Just kidding, Mom," I say. "But I'll admit, my life is quite full."

She gives me this deeply caring look. Suddenly, tears are spilling over her double set of false lashes and smearing the Cleopatra liner around her cat green eyes.

Mom reaches out and strokes my cheek. Her hands are warm. They smell like bread. "Clueless," she says softly.

* * *

I'm not saying that dream changed my life.

Nothing earth-shattering happened when I woke. I was in the usual fog of frantic loss I'm always in after a dream about Mom. Like, whoa, where'd she go? Where am I? I mean, I never even knew her. So you'd think, well, how can I miss her? But through the years, she keeps showing up in these dreams. And when I wake, I have to get used to her not being here all over again.

Totally not a big deal. I mean, when I looked around, I was in my ordinary king-size canopied bed, wrapped in regulation sleepwear: a T-shirt and boy's boxers. To tell the truth, by the time I finished brushing my teeth and started yanking the squiggly rods out of my hair, I was over it. Whatever Mom meant had whizzed by me.

My entire wardrobe is programmed into my computer. I flipped it on and started scanning the racks for an appropriate ensemble. It was report card day, so I was after a sensitive, studenty kind of thing.

The lemon cashmere sweater I chose was way scholastic and excellently set off my long blond hair. Blue tones in the plaid mini and matching vest brought out the azure in my eyes. Accessories can make or break a look, so at the last minute I added a pale beret and silk thigh highs.

Although everyone assures me I'm a genuine babe, I wouldn't say I'm brutally gorgeous. But I *so* know how to accessorize. A final spin before the mirror convinced me I'd hit the winning combo. I looked academic yet stylish; deserving of excellent grades, yet humble. Mission accomplished, I descended the stairs.

I live in Beverly Hills with my father, who is a totally prominent attorney. Daddy wasn't down yet, so I went out back to pick some breakfast oranges.

We have acres of land with practically a fruit market growing on trees. And I'm fully responsible for running the homestead. I handle all the help. I like to kid around with them. So that morning I threw an orange at José, our gardener. As I was heading back to the house, I felt something whiz past my cheek and a second later heard a pane of extremely expensive beveled glass shatter. José likes to kid around, too.

Back inside, I saw my dad coming down the stairs. Our maid, Lucy, saw him, too, and scurried out of sight. Lucy has gained twenty pounds since she came to work for us. She was never exactly a petite. She says she eats out of nerves. My father makes her nervous.

Lucy thinks that if my dad realizes we have a maid, he'll demand that she work or fire her. So she tries to hide when he's at home, and eats when he's not. Also Lucy colors her own hair. It's this glowing red shade not found in nature, with about an inch of black roots showing most of the time. Some inner rhythm tells Lucy when it's time for a touch-up. It's just as well my father doesn't see her much. He's like very into neatness and grooming.

Anyway, Lucy scurried into her room, and my dad came downstairs.

"Good morning," I said with a cheery smile and a toss of my long, subtly highlighted hair. I offered him a glass of freshly squeezed orange juice.

"Cher, don't start that again," Daddy growled. He is totally unconscious about his own health and welfare.

Daddy was wearing the new shirt I'd gotten him, but his tie, which I'd also picked out, was unknotted. He started buttoning his vest, then came toward me with his chin lifted, and I did this extremely professional tie knot for him. It's just one of the things Daddy counts on me for. Since Mom died, I'm really all he has—although it's true this absolute horde of Bettys has passed through our lives.

Dad even married some of them. His shortest marriage, six weeks, was to Nicole, a practically bionic actress who had like maybe zero left on her entire body that hadn't been surgically improved. She even had lipo on her ankles. Other than my mom, his longest marriage was to Gail. That lasted a huge three years. Gail came complete with a child, my former stepbrother, Josh.

I am almost sixteen. That would make Josh nineteen now. My friends used to think he was *so* cute, *three* years older than us and a real Baldwin. I thought Josh was a serious pain. He was always trying to take care of me. Which I totally hate! I have been taking care of myself, and of Daddy and Lucy and lots of my friends, too, for years and years. I didn't need the Ralph Nader of stepsiblings trying to cushion life's blows for me. But Josh was all, "Oh, Cher, you never had a mother . . ." And, of course, I *so* appreciate a refresher course on my own heritage.

My mom was the all-time winner, though. I think Dad just never found anyone he loved as much as her. Even Josh said that. The best thing about Josh was that he was wild about Daddy, who is not just your regular lovable old dad.

Daddy is a litigator. That's the kind of lawyer that does the meanest fighting. My dad is so good, he gets five hundred dollars an hour, but he fights with me for free because I'm his daughter.

I followed him into the kitchen. *"Daddy, you need vitamin C."*

"Where's my briefcase?" he asked, his bushy black eyebrows scrunched in concentration as he looked around the room.

I handed him his briefcase. "And don't try to sneak out of the office," I warned. "Dr. Lovett's nurse is coming by to give you a flu shot."

"Where are my keys?" he demanded. They were on top of the microwave. I got them for him.

"Josh just got into town from Seattle. He's coming over for dinner," he said.

"Oh, no! Why?"

"He's your stepbrother, Cher," Daddy said.

"Oh, please. You were hardly married to his mother, and that was five years ago," I reminded him. "Why do I have to see Josh?"

"You divorce wives, not children," he explained.

I offered him the juice again. "Forget it," he said, and left.

I drank the juice myself. "You can come out now, Lucy," I called.

Lucy's evil dye job appeared at the door. "He's gone?" she asked. When I nodded yes, she clumped into the kitchen, the rubber soles of her orthopedic shoes squeaking on the terrazzo tiles.

Lucy is my special friend, although she's centuries older. I thought a perky little uniform would do wonders for her appearance and her disposition. So I got her this adorable domestic ensemble I saw at a Beverly Hills uniform boutique. But the white ruffled French apron tied around her shiny black uniform now looked like a bib on a truck.

"Want some juice?" I offered.

"Are you kidding? I read an orange has eighty calories and a glass of juice has at least three oranges," Lucy said indignantly.

"Lucy, I told you, calories don't count. You've got to raise your metabolic thermostat."

"My thermostat is fine," Lucy said, throwing wide the double doors of the designer fridge and taking stock of the contents. "My butt is the problem."

I tossed an orange into my pony-hide back-pack and gave Lucy a wave. "We'll discuss it later," I said, grabbing my books. "I'm Audi."

I picked Dionne up in the totally loqued-out Jeep Daddy bought me. It had four-wheel drive and a monster sound system. I didn't have a license yet, but I needed something to learn on.

Whoops, pretend that didn't happen, I told myself as, rounding the gracious curve of De's driveway, the Jeep's awesome grille snagged a loose piece of lawn furniture.

Dionne and I are named for famous singers of our parents' generation. De is an AA goddess. That's AA as in African American, not Alcoholics Anonymous, which is the total rage with my friends' parents. De and I are practically insepa-rable. We're like mirror-image sisters. De's hair is all long and dark and threaded through with excellent extensions. Mine is long and blond, and it was even before Sergio, my hairdresser, talked me into highlights. And De's got these killer black eyes with double rows of totally natural lashes that make guys stutter.

Dionne lives with her mom in this quaint Tudor mansion. De's mom is one of the premier PR women in LA. That's PR as in public rela-tions. Her clients include soap stars, heads of little countries, and one of the nation's top-rated talk show hosts. Dionne's mother is practically as famous as her clients. She's called Carolina. Everyone calls her that, even De. She travels all the time. But they've got a fabu housekeeper named Melba, who's like a total other mom to Dionne.

De and I share a rampant interest in fashion. That morning she was wearing a whimsical outfit with a tall top hat. "Dude!" she greeted me, climbing into the Jeep.

"Girlfriend!" I cried. We did our Beverly Hills high five, raising our palms, then deliberately missing each other's hands, and ending with a limp-wristed slap.

"Have you been shopping with Dr. Seuss?" I asked, peering over my shades at her hat.

She cocked her head at my pony fur bag. "At least I wouldn't skin my collie to make a back-pack," she said.

We laughed. "It's faux," I reassured her, glid-ing by a red road sign.

"Hello," said Dionne. "That was a Stop sign."

"Please," I said, "I totally paused."

De goes out with Murray, who wears huge baggy Calvins and a do-rag on his head. He's like very *GQ*, into the foremost urban togs major plastic can purchase. Murray drives a BMW and writes rap songs about career choices, invest-ments, foreign car maintenance, and other prob-lems he's facing.

I spotted him beeping the alarm on his Beemer as Dionne and I started across the school court-yard—which at Beverly Hills High is called the Quad. It's landscaped to the max and arrayed with top-quality stone fountains, benches, and other attractive lounging possibilities, including an outdoor dining area.

Before I even got to tell De that Murray was in the vicinity, her pager went off.

"Murray's beeping me already," she said, without even checking her pager. "I mean it's not even eight-thirty."

"He's so possessive," I sympathized.

"It's like he called last night, and he's all, 'Where were you today?' and I'm all, 'What do you think? At my grandmother's' and he's all—"

I rolled my eyes and tuned De out. She's in this dramatic relationship with Murray. I think they were overly influenced by the Ike and Tina Turner movie.

"De, why do you put up with it?" I said when she paused for a vital breath. "You can do so much better."

"Oh, no, here he comes." Dionne sighed as Murray approached in embarrassingly low-slung jeans.

"Woman, why didn't you answer my page?"

De cringed. "I *hate* when you call me woman."

"Where you been all weekend?" Murray demanded as kids began to gather around to hear the fight. "You jeepin' behind my back?"

Dionne started digging through her bag. "Jeepin'?" she said in this dangerously controlled voice. "No, but speaking of vehicular excitement . . ." Triumphantly, she pulled a shiny length of braided black hair out of her bag.

"Perhaps you can explain how this cheap K Mart hair extension got into your backseat?"

"Eeeyew, what's that?" one of the gathered spectators shrieked. "Yeah," another one of the group demanded, turning to Murray. "Tell her, man. Where'd it come from?"

Murray pulled himself up. "I don't know nothing about that," he said. "That must have come off of you."

"Bhaaaap!" Someone did a buzzer sound and said, "Wrong! Try again, bro."

Dionne said, "Tscha! I do not wear shiny, polyester hair, unlike some people, like, say . . . Shawana."

"Ooooo," said the crowd.

Murray's head started bobbing like one of those tacky backseat dogs. "Sha-wa-na??" He was outraged. "Man, you should get a job at the Fox Network. You have a real talent for fabrication. Shawana!"

"That's right, Shawana," Dionne insisted. "And anytime you decide you'd rather be with that anorexic bimbette, instead of a woman who's t.b., true blue, just pull up your saggy Calvins and go."

I backed away as they continued. "Dionne," I called, "I'm Audi. See you later."

De took time out to wave good-bye to me, then went back to her emotional moment. Which surprised no one since at least once a day Dionne and Murray entertain everyone with a dramatic improv. It's made them immensely popular. All the kids know De and Murray; people take sides, discussion groups form during lunch.

Personally, I thought, as I made my way across the Quad, I can't imagine going out with a high school boy. They're so high maintenance. Like dogs. You have to walk them, feed them, practically give them flea baths, just so you can have some nervous creature jump and slobber all over you.

Unfortunately, high school boys are the only guys you meet in high school. So I hadn't exactly had a serious boyfriend yet. But I thought it was better to wait than to lower my standards. Anyway, I'd sublimated my excess energy into my schoolwork.

Chapter 2

Should all oppressed people be allowed refuge in America?" Mr. Hall asked.

Amber Salk and I were in front of the class with him. We were standing behind podiums, getting ready to debate. Mr. Hall was leaning against his desk.

Mr. Hall's okay. He's maybe a little shorter than my father, like a foot. He's also hair-impaired, with this little perfect bald spot on top of his head. He's mostly very reasonable. And tolerant. And overworked. He's like a teacher poster boy. He loses it once in a while, but primarily he's got an excellent attitude.

Which is more than anyone can say about Amber, who is deeply renowned for her negativity. So it seemed fitting when Mr. Hall said,

"Cher will take the pro position, and Amber will be con. Okay, Cher, you begin."

I cleared my throat and tried to clear my head. Mr. Hall was very into current events. His classroom was papered with depressing true stories he'd snipped from news magazines. On the board behind him was a photo essay on Haitian refugees. It was way inspirational.

"So, okay. Like right now the Haitians need to come to America," I began. I'd actually given this debate some thought. "But some people are all, 'What about the strain on our resources?' And it's like when I had this garden party for my father's birthday and it's all catered, you know, I said RSVP because it's a sit-down dinner, okay?"

Mr. Hall's head tilted over to the right, and his teeny blue eyes got all squinched up like he was straining to get what I was saying. I gave him an encouraging smile, and continued.

"People come that like didn't RSVP! And I'm buggin'. I have to like race to the kitchen, redistribute the food, and like squish in extra place settings. And people are on mismatched chairs and all. But by the end of the day it was like 'the more, the merrier.'"

I could tell by the way Mr. Hall was looking at me that he needed the conclusion spelled out. "And so, if the government could just get to the kitchen and rearrange some things, we could certainly party with the Haitians. And in conclusion, may I remind you that it doesn't say RSVP on the Statue of Liberty."

14

Well, the entire class, minus Amber and Mr. Hall, started whooping and applauding. But at least Mr. Hall nodded intelligently. He totally got what I was saying. "All right. Now, Amber. Reply," he said.

Amber was furiously flustered. "Mr. Hall," she whined, "the topic is refugees, and she's talking about some little party."

I gasped. "It was his fiftieth birthday! There were like two hundred people."

"What*ever,*" said Amber, giving her big hair a flip. "If she doesn't do the assignment, I can't do mine."

"Oh, take an Advil, Amber," I said.

"Ladies, cool it," Mr. Hall warned.

Behind his back, Amber gave the class a sarcastic look, like "Cool It"?! just because he used this archaeological phrase.

"Cher is obviously using her father's birthday as a metaphor for political asylum," Mr. Hall explained to her. He was unbelievably on target. "Your job is to find flaws in her argument. I can't believe you don't see any."

Amber made a *W* with her fingers, for what*ever.*

"Does anyone have any thoughts on Cher's oration?" Hall asked the class.

To my surprise Elton Lozoff, who's rampantly popular and excellently attractive for a high school boy, raised his hand. I didn't think he'd heard anything I said. He'd been organizing his CDs during my talk.

"Elton," Mr. Hall said. "Comments?"

Elton's brow furrowed with concern. "Mr. Hall, I can't find my Smashing Pumpkins," he said. "Can I go to the Quad and look before someone snags it?"

"You may certainly not," Mr. Hall said, ignoring the evil eye Elton shot him. "Any further insights?"

Travis Birkenstock—long-haired space traveler —raised his hand. Mr. Hall looked amazed.

"I had an insight," Travis said. With a slow, goofy smile, he flicked back his dubiously blond hair.

"I'm all ears," said Mr. Hall.

"Well, like, the way I feel about the Rolling Stones is like the way my kids will feel about Nine Inch Nails." Travis blinked earnestly. "So I shouldn't torment my mother anymore about them."

Mr. Hall blinked back at Travis. "Yes . . . well, it's a little off the subject of Haiti, but tolerance is always a good lesson, even when it comes out of nowhere."

Travis beamed proudly until Mr. Hall continued: "With that in mind, I'll distribute your report cards." Then Travis and the whole class sort of groaned and slumped down in their seats, and everyone started whispering and talking.

"Quiet, please," Mr. Hall said as he walked through the aisles handing out cards. "Is there a

Christian Stovitz enrolled in this class? Has anyone ever seen him?"

I waved my hand. "Mr. Hall, I never met the boy, but the buzz on Christian is that his parents have joint custody. And he's like supposed to spend one semester in Chicago and one semester here. Personally," I added, "I think it's a travesty on the part of the legal profession."

"Thank you for that perspective, Cher." Mr. Hall cleared his throat and threw a fierce glance at Paroudasm Banafshein, who was holding court at the back of the room. Parou was ranting to his pals in furiously audible Farsi. The glare from his gold Rolex bounced off their snickering faces.

"Can *all* conversations come to a halt," Mr. Hall said pointedly, "including Farsi, English, Japanese, Spanish . . ."

He handed Travis his report card. Travis took one look at it, walked to the window, and started to climb out. Mr. Hall grabbed the back of Travis's oversize vintage green Izod and hauled him back. "And can suicide attempts wait until next period, please?"

He gave me my report card just as the bell rang. "May I remind you," he announced with a total lack of sensitivity, "these must be signed by tomorrow."

I dialed Dionne on my cellular the minute I hit the hall. Some kids were leaning against their lockers, dejectedly staring at their report cards. There were little support groups of students clumped all over the place, consoling one another. But for the most part it was chaos as usual. I made my way briskly through the crush, holding my head high—as high as I could while cradling my cellular, anyway.

"Zup?" Dionne's voice came through the phone crackle.

"You get your report card?"

"Yeah," De said. "I'm toast. You'll never see me out of the house again. What about you?"

Elton passed surrounded by fans. He waved a CD in my direction. "Smashing Pumpkins. I found it," he called, grinning triumphantly.

"Report card," I called to him. "How'd you make out?"

He stuck a finger in his mouth and pantomimed hurling.

"That good?"

"What?" De said.

"No, I was just saying that to Elton."

"So how did you do?"

"Grades? I totally choked. My father's going to go postal on me."

"Tell me about it. Mr. Hall was way harsh," De said. "I got a C minus in debate."

I turned a corner and crashed into her. "He gave me a C," I continued, folding the cellular. "Which drags down my whole average."

De opened the quilted black leather bag that had eaten her AmEx balance and tucked away her phone. We were at the door to her next class. "Unfair," she commiserated.

"Furiously," I agreed. We did a limper than usual high five, and she went in.

"See ya."

"I'll call you," I said, unfolding my cellular. I turned the corner, stopped in front of Miss Geist's class, and dialed De.

Dusk was falling, or whatever. I pulled the Jeep into our cobbled circular driveway and just sat there for a minute, staring at the house. It's way decent. My father bought it minutes before I was born for only eight hundred thousand. Now it's worth at least two mill. Daddy makes monster investments. He's so financial.

It was supposed to be this cozy love nest for the three of us—me, him, and Mom. Sometimes I wonder what that would have been like. She was around long enough to see me walk and hear me say "Mama." That's all I know. Daddy and I hardly ever talk about her. He's way emotional. And with his cholesterol level, I try not to introduce potentially upsetting topics of a personal nature.

What would it be like if she were inside waiting for me right now, I wondered, sitting there in the Jeep I'd described to her in my dream. Would Lucy cook more nutritional meals if my mom were supervising her? Would Daddy be healthier? Would he be happier? Would she like me? I felt way tired suddenly. I shut my eyes tightly, then opened them wide and took a deep breath. Anyway, I do a fully excellent job at the helm of the household, I reminded myself. Then I slung my knapsack over my shoulder and went inside.

Crossing the living room, I passed the portrait of Mom in full disco gear. I don't actually remember her at all, but I like to pretend she's watching me. "Ma," I said, pulling out a test paper from last week and waving it at the painting. "Look, ninety-eight in geometry. Pretty groovy, right?"

A noise from the kitchen distracted me. Bad music. The kind that was playing when the dinosaurs went down. Woodstock nation. Josh was back.

"Yuck! What is it about college and crybaby music?" I asked, bouncing into the kitchen.

My father's most recent ex-wife's son was behind the refrigerator door, foraging for food. I couldn't see his face, but the frayed cuffs of his hopelessly outdated jeans were enough for me to make a positive ID.

"Hey, Cher. Who's watching the Galleria?" he quipped, honoring me with a full frontal smile. Josh's teeth are rampantly fine. Totally rehabilitated. And they only cost Daddy twenty-two thou in braces and maintenance. Now, like his teeth, Josh straightened up.

He looked taller than I remembered. Tanner, too. I was surprised at how wide his shoulders were—no doubt a souvenir of time spent with his mom and latest stepdad in lumberjack land. His taste hadn't improved, though.

"So the flannel shirt deal, what is that?" I asked. "Is it like a nod to the crisp Seattle weather . . . or to keep you warm as you stand guard over the refrigerator?" I strolled over to close the door he'd left open.

Josh's smile broadened, and he started to tickle me. "Hey . . . you're filling out there."

"Hey . . . your face is catching up with your mouth," I said, twirling out of his reach.

"I went by Dad's office."

"He's not your dad," I reminded him. "Your dad split ages ago. *My* dad just happened to marry your mother *briefly*. We are not related, Josh, get it? Why don't you torture your new family?"

"Just because my mom is married to someone else now, doesn't mean I don't still think of Mel as a father," he said.

I headed for the den. Josh followed me. "I hope you're not thinking of staying here," I said over my shoulder.

"Nope. I got a place in Westwood near school."

Oh, no, Josh had transferred to UCLA. There went the neighborhood. I flicked on the TV. He collapsed onto the couch. *Beavis and Butthead* was on. "Wouldn't it be better if you went to college back East?" I suggested. "They say girls at NYU aren't at all particular."

He grabbed the remote and switched to CNN.

"You just got here and already you're playing Couch Commando?" I switched back to MTV.

"You know, in some parts of the universe— maybe not in Contempo Casuals—but in some parts, it's considered cool to know what's going on in the world."

It was déjà vu all over again. Josh had returned to better my life. I stuffed the remote down between the couch cushions, out of his reach. "Oh, thank you, Josh," I said. "I *so* need lessons from you on how to be cool. Tell me the part about Kenny G. again."

Daddy's voice entirely squelched any retort. "Hey, you two chuckleheads, get in here. Dinner's ready," he called.

Chuckleheads?! What was that? The Litigator was turning into Sitcom Dad. I couldn't help noticing that my father's affection for Josh seemed to have a mellowing effect on him. Josh laughed. I squinched up my eyes at him. We joined Daddy for dinner.

"Josh, are you still growing?" Daddy asked as we were sitting down. "You look taller than you did at Easter."

"I don't think so, Mel," Josh said.

Dad turned to me. "Doesn't Josh look bigger?"

"His head does."

"So how's your mother?" Daddy asked him.

"Putting on weight," Josh responded.

Dad brightened. "Really? Glad to hear it.

Have you been thinking about our little discussion on corporate law?"

"Sure," Josh said. "But I'd really love to check out environmental law."

"What for?" Daddy snapped. "You want to have a frustrating, miserable life?"

"Josh will have that no matter what he does," I suggested.

They totally ignored me.

"Also, Mel," Josh continued, "I was wondering about criminal law."

Daddy's thick black eyebrows practically bumped into each other. He shook his head. "No, no, no, that's sleazy. It's not like on TV. You want to be doing something decent, something lucrative!"

Josh's smile wavered. He looked kind of on the verge of hurt. My dad was turning dangerously red. I jumped in to quell the conflict. "Daddy, he's not even in law school yet," I quickly pointed out.

"At least Josh knows what he wants to do, and he's in a good college." My father waved his fork at me. There was a chunk of broiled red cholesterol at the end of it. He hadn't eaten a leaf of the salad I'd specifically asked Lucy to prepare. And the puddle of grease on his baked potato did not look like I Can't Believe It's Not Butter. "I'd like to see you have a little direction," he grumbled.

"I have direction."

"Yeah"—Josh laughed—"toward the mall."

Great, I thought. Remind me to try saving Josh from Daddy's temper again sometime.

"Okay, okay, you two." It was the return of sitcom Dad. Suddenly, my father was chuckling. Clearly, Josh's remark had amused him. "By the way, Cher, that reminds me. Where's your report card?"

I sat tall in my chair. "It's not ready yet."

"What do you mean?"

"Well, some teachers were trying to lowball me, Daddy, and you always say, 'Never accept a first offer.' I figure these grades are just a jumping-off point to start negotiations. I'll have something for you to see by the end of the week."

A telephone rang. Daddy, Josh, and I all checked our cellulars. It was for Daddy. I was relieved when he pushed away his steak plate and started talking contracts over the phone.

"You are so pathetic," I hissed at Josh.

"And you're a superficial space cadet. What makes you think you can get teachers to change your grades?"

I sent a squinchie of triumph in his direction. "Only the fact that I've done it every other semester," I said.

Chapter 3

The next day I hit Beverly Hills High with a vengeance. I had told Josh I could get my grades changed. Now it was time to prove it.

It took exactly thirteen minutes, by the clock on the locker room wall, to get Ms. Stoeger, my PE teacher, to upgrade me. I shed a few tears and told her an undeserving male had broken my heart. She raised my C to a B after we agreed all men were pigs.

Miss Geist, the history teacher, went along with the program. We had an important meeting of the minds on industrial waste. I nodded emphatically while she unburdened her heart on the subject. When she took a breath, I pledged to start a letter-writing campaign to my congressman about violations of the Clean Air Act. Presto, B plus.

Mr. Hall, however, was totally rigid. I reviewed for him my homework, reports, and other evidence of continuous and genuine effort. He was unmoved. He claimed my debates were unresearched, unstructured, and unconvincing. As if! I became humiliatingly humble. In desperation, I tried cleaning the blackboard, begging, and arguing. Mr. Hall remained inflexible. Years of molding young minds had taught him how to be cold.

I left his classroom fighting back an unfamiliar panic. I could practically hear Josh's laughter ringing in my ears. Worse yet, I could imagine my father's reaction. With his cholesterol count, massive rage was the last thing he needed. Also I could lose my Jeep.

Feeling impotent and out of control, which I totally hate, I needed to find sanctuary. I needed a place where I could gather my thoughts and regain my strength. I beeped Dionne and told her to meet me at the mall.

The Beverly Center, with its fountains, trees, and ATM machines, distracted me for a while. I picked up this raging Versace bustier; De got her nose pierced. We were bent, loaded down with packages, in a matter of hours. We took a break on a bench outside Banana Republic.

"Wassup, Cher?" De said gently. "Are you suffering from buyer's remorse?"

"As if! But we've been shopping all day, and I

still don't know what to do about Mr. Hall," I admitted. "I tried everything to convince him of my scholastic aptitude and was brutally rebuffed."

Dionne tried to cheer me up. "He's just a miserable little man who wants everyone else to be miserable, too."

"De, that's it," I said. "We've got to figure out how to make Mr. Hall sublimely happy."

Dionne rolled her eyes. "No, seriously, girl," I said. "Think about it. Here's this lonely little man, loaded down with books and papers, schlepping through crowds of intense students every day—most of whom drive better cars than his. I mean, here's the stats on Mr. Hall. He's single, he's forty-two, and he earns minor wages at a thankless job. What that man needs is a good, healthy relationship!"

"Cher, are you buggin'?" Dionne said. "You're going to date Mr. Hall?"

"Earth alert! De, I'm just going to set the wheels in motion."

The next day I ran a quick check on the teachers' cafeteria. What I saw was an assortment of unattractive women. Even makeover potential was limited. Unfortunately, there was a serious babe drought among the teachers.

The blue-haired Miss Wimmer and Miss Taylor were sharing a copy of *Modern Maturity* and picking at the white bread sandwiches they'd brought from home. They were hardly age appropriate. Then there were the evil trolls from the math department, Harding and Hanratty. They were both actually married. Ms. Stoeger sat at a table apart, alone with her yogurt. In the grand tradition of PE teachers, she had a tattoo and no great fondness for those of the male persuasion. The sole femme of the history department, Miss Geist, was mindlessly spilling coffee down the front of her blouse. There it joined a full menu of dribbles du jour.

Still, something told me not to discount Miss Geist.

I studied her during fifth period. Elton was sitting behind me. He gave me a neck rub, while Geist scrawled a massive weekend homework assignment on the blackboard. She was as oblivious to the groaning students behind her as she was to the coffee and other groceries on her chest.

Still, she had potential. She had chipmunk cheeks and totally undisciplined dark curly hair, which she tried to control with plastic barrettes. Her pale eyes were massively magnified by glasses that constantly slid down her nose. But she was somewhere around Mr. Hall's age and somewhere around Mr. Hall's height, and when she wasn't slouching, you could see she had an actual waistline.

Sure, she had lipstick on her teeth, her stockings were full of runs, and she'd been having bad hair days since September. But Mr. Hall might respond. It would be uphill, but it was definitely doable.

If Hall could see me doing my homework now, I thought. It was way past bedtime. Yet there I was, sprawled across the king-size, copying out a poem, like an actual student. There were piles of books around me and about a gazillion squished pieces of yellow legal-pad paper on the bed.

I'd practiced Mr. Hall's handwriting on those crumpled pages. From the comments he'd made in the margins of my homework, I had massive samplings of his large, loopy scrawl. Now, with one of Daddy's beautifully marbled Montblanc pens, I carefully mimicked Mr. Hall's wide *O*'s and *A*'s and the fat stems of his *T*'s and *L*'s until the verse was complete.

The next morning I checked the poem for telltale spelling errors a final time. De beeped me as I pulled into the school parking lot. "Meet me outside the office," I told her. "And snag a rose off the Quad on the way."

We were on a mission. We needed to glide obscurely into and out of the administration office. I had dressed down in a simple black-and-gray micro-mini and bare-belly blazer. De, on the other hand, decided to camouflage herself as a Vegas slot machine.

"Could your hat be bigger or redder, please?" I asked outside the office.

"Did you get your colors done and find out your season is Death?" she shot back.

We peeked in the window. Traffic was light. The school secretary was in front of her computer, checking the Personals on the Internet. Everyone else must have been in the teachers' lounge, smoking their brains out and swigging Listerine.

De and I walked in and went right to the student activities bulletin board. It was next to the teachers' mailboxes. We perused the board casually.

"Let me see the note," De said. I passed it to her. " 'Rough winds do shake the darling buds of May, And summer's lease has all too short a date, But thy eternal summer shall not fade . . .' Phat, Cher! Did you write that?"

"Duh! It's like a famous quote."

"From where?"

"Cliff's Notes," I explained, putting the note and the rose in Miss Geist's box.

"But 'Secret Admirer'? Why didn't you sign Mr. Hall's name?"

"This is just to get her used to the idea of being liked. Start her endorphins going."

De and I ducked behind a corner. A second later, in clunked Geist. She was dressed in drab with her usual wildly spiraling nest of hair. Stuck into it, like those shiny objects birds bring home in TV nature specials, were two barrettes and a pencil. She went directly to the teachers' boxes. With her all-purpose blank stare, she saw the rose, plucked out the note, and read it. A smile dimpled her chipmunk cheeks.

"Cher, she actually looked happy!" Dionne squealed when Geist had gone.

"Classic," I said.

De dropped me off at Mr. Hall's class. Amber Salk, fashion victim, plunked herself down in front of me. Her vinyl skirt was okay. The actual leopard-skin belt, however, was a blast from the ecological past. Ricki Lake would've picketed her. In keeping with the wilderness theme, Amber's hair was all Kingdom of the Frizzies.

"How about a French braid?" I suggested.

"Return with the dinosaurs to 1992," she said.

"What did *you* have in mind?"

Amber shrugged. "Work on it." She pulled a bag of beauty supplies out of her backpack and plunked them down on my desk.

"Are there scissors in here?" I asked.

"Don't get extreme."

While I styled Amber, Travis studied his skateboard, looking for sticker vacancies. Elton was mumbling into his cellular. And Mr. Hall was handing out tardies.

"Paroudasm Banafshein?" he called.

"Here," said the Iranian prince.

"Sixteen tardies to work off."

Paroudasm let loose a rant of way harsh Farsi insults. His loyal subjects in the back row laughed.

Mr. Hall rose above it. "Janet Hong, no tardies," he continued. "Travis Birkenstock, congratulations. By far the most tardies in the class. Thirty-eight in all. A near-perfect record."

The class did an Arsenio—waving and whooping as Travis, skateboard tucked under his arm, stood up to take a bow. His hair flopped forward.

"Thank you, thank you." He was all grinning gladness. "This is so unexpected. I didn't even have a speech prepared. . . . But I would like to say this . . . tardiness is not something you can do all on your own. Many, many people had to contribute. I'd like to thank my parents for never driving me to school. And the LA bus drivers for taking a chance on an unknown kid. And last but not least, the wonderful crew at McDonald's for the long hours they spend making Egg McMuffins, without which I might never be tardy. Thank you."

Everyone applauded. Travis sat back down. Mr. Hall shook his head. "Well, if Mr. Birkenstock has no further acknowledgments to include in his speech, I'll go on. Cher Horowitz, two tardies."

I stood up. Amber shrieked. I realized I was still holding her hair. I dropped her split ends and said, "I object, Mr. Hall. I have never been tardy."

Mr. Hall closed his eyes as if in prayer. "Cher, does everything have to be a negotiation with you?"

"Do you recall the dates of the alleged tardies?" I asked.

"One was last Monday."

"Mr. Hall, did you taste the vegetarian chili in the Quad on Monday? Half the school was hurling in the lounges. I was deadly ill."

"All right. I'll let one of them slide."

"Thanks, Mr. Hall," I said. "Miss Geist was right about you."

"What do you mean?"

"Miss Geist said you were the only one in this school with any compassion."

The class went "Oooooo."

"Really?" Mr. Hall said, tilting his adorable bald head. "Miss Geist said that?"

Chapter 4

When I got home that afternoon, I could've sworn Disco Mom winked at me as I passed her portrait. The plan was cooking. Elton Lozoff, Murray, and a bunch of other gangsta wannabes had a clique they called the Crew. I decided to recruit them to help me drop hints between Geist and Hall.

I beeped Elton at the recording studio he called his bedroom. He had a rotating black leather recliner in it that gave him easy access to his state-of-the-art audio equipment and CD racks.

"Elton, you've got to work with me on this," I explained.

"Hold on, this music's too in your face," he said. "Let's go with something more mellow."

While he browsed through his CD collection, I carried the cellular to the kitchen. There was a mixing bowl and a soup spoon in the sink. The bottom of the bowl was grunged with the remains of a hefty banana split. In a half inch of dishwater, a couple of browning banana slices floated with a froth of melted ice cream, hot fudge smears, and a confetti of rainbow sprinkles. Lucy's lunch. I rinsed out the dish while I waited for Elton.

His return was announced by a blast of Massive Attack. "Okay, where were we?"

"You know how open-minded people are when they're in love," I said.

"In love," he repeated. "Why didn't you say so. Mmmm . . . I think some Coolio would be good. . . ."

"Elton, I appreciate the value of a good background sound track as much as anyone, but would you listen to me for a minute."

It was too late. He was off again. I fixed myself a snack—No-Cal soda, nonfat ice cream, and a sprinkle of Sweet 'n Low. Then Elton was back with Coolio behind him.

"There we go. Now, you were saying?"

"Elton! Are you spacing or what? Listen, I'll give you things for people to say. You see that they say them. Then it's Aceville for all of us."

"Achievable," he said.

"Great. Peace." I hung up.

"Cher! Get in here!"

Uh-oh, Daddy was home. I followed the bellowing to his office. His face was all telltale red. His eyebrows were like a single angry slash across his forehead. Even his nose hairs were quivering.

I gave him a big, bright smile. "Hi, Daddy!" A perky, upbeat attitude is very important to a successful negotiation. I suspected that there might be some serious bargaining to be done here.

"Do you know what this is about?" Daddy waved a letter in my face. I glanced at it.

"A second notice for three outstanding tickets. Gee, I don't remember a first notice."

"The *ticket* is the first notice," he explained. "I didn't even know you could get tickets before you have a license."

"Oh, sure," I said helpfully. "You can get tickets anytime."

"Is that so? Well, not around here you can't. From now on you don't drive, sit, or breathe on that Jeep unless you're with a licensed driver. And no cruising around with Dionne!" he added. "Two permits do not equal a license. Do I make myself clear?"

It was hard to keep smiling, but I did. I felt the throat-thickening, nose-tickling, eyes-stinging warning signs of tears. But it's important to stay positive in every situation. So I kept smiling and said, "Yes, Daddy."

"I expect you to be a good driver. I want to see you apply yourself to something besides make-up."

"I will, Daddy," I promised. "I'm going to practice hard."

I was relieved that his face was returning to pasty and that a reasonable space had begun to part his eyebrows. Healthwise, he's not supposed to rave all that much.

I left Daddy's office and went in search of Josh. I spotted his oiled pecs broiling in the sun. They looked surprisingly sturdy, as if old Josh had whiled away his dreary Seattle days pumping iron. He was reading, of course, stretched out beside the pool. I slipped into a lounge chair near him. "Hey, granola breath, you've got something on your chin," I said cheerfully.

"I'm growing a goatee," he said, without looking up from his book.

"Oh, good. You don't want to be the last one at the coffeehouse without slacker fuzz."

Finally, he closed this weighty hardcover and shot me a limp grin. "I can't tell you how much I enjoy these little chats of ours, Cher. But in the interest of saving time, why don't you just tell me what you want."

"Okay. So, actually, I have a permit, and I know how to drive and all. But Daddy said I can only take the Jeep out with a licensed driver. Besides, don't you want to take a break from"— I checked the book cover, looked at the author's name—"from . . . whatever," I said.

"Nietzsche," he instructed me.

"Nietzsche. No kidding. What's it about?"

"Everything" was his debonair answer.

"Boy, college is vague."

"It's not for college," Josh said.

"As if! You're reading a book that's not even required? Proper!"

Josh set down the book and got up reluctantly. "What are the chances you'll shut up till you get your way?"

It was a good question. I thought about it. "Slim to none," I told him.

"Okay." He grabbed his shirt and pulled it on as we strolled around front to the Jeep.

I did a perfect reverse out of the driveway. We didn't hit one thing. I was thinking how impressed Josh must be when suddenly he became a total squirrel. It was all over a wide turn I made. We didn't graze one palm tree, but Josh shot me this look like, *You idiot.* Of course, that did absolute wonders for my confidence.

He was way nervous, gripping the seats, checking the side mirrors. I tried to calm him by kidding around. The next time I scraped the curb, I gave him my best grin and said, "Whee?"

"Cher, see those lines painted on the road?"

"Uh-huh."

"Well, pick a pair and stay inside them."

"I am," I said. "You try driving in platforms!" He was seriously rattling me. The next thing I knew, I'd overadjusted the wheel, and we veered over the center line and were practically facing oncoming traffic.

"Look out," Josh hollered. He leaned across

me and turned the wheel, then slammed his foot on the brake. "Cher, keep your eyes on the road. Not the houses, not the billboards, not the store windows, just the road!" He was hollering like a guy who'd let his Librium prescription run out.

I felt terrible. What was going on? All the males around me were having a breakdown fest. "You don't have to jump on top of me!" I hollered right back.

"I'm trying to keep us alive. Believe me, I have no desire to jump on you."

I didn't know whether I was scared, hurt, or angry. I could feel tears creeping up on me again. I decided to go safe—with angry. "Then move off me! Move over to your side, Josh."

He did. We glared at each other for a minute, then I started the car up again.

"Listen, I have to get back to school. Do you want to practice parking?" he asked after he'd cooled out. I could tell he was trying to make up.

"What's the point? Everywhere you go has valet parking."

Josh shook his head, and after that he didn't say much. I broke the ice. "So what class are you going to?"

"Actually, I'm going to a Tree People meeting. We might get Marky Mark to plant a celebrity tree."

I couldn't help being sarcastic. "How fabulous! You're getting Marky Mark to pull up his Calvins and plant a tree?" Then I thought about it. It sounded really stupid. I mean, what did Marky

Mark know about trees? "Why don't you just hire gardeners who at least know what they're doing?" I asked.

Josh went minorly ballistic. "Maybe Marky Mark wants to use his popularity for a good cause," he growled. "Maybe he wants to make a contribution. In case you've never heard of it, a contribution is the giving of time or funds to assist a needy person or cause."

"Excuse me, but I have donated many Italian shoes to Lucy," I pointed out. "And when I get my license, I fully intend to brake for animals. And I'm contributing many hours helping two lonely teachers find romance."

"Which I'll bet serves your interests more than theirs." He shook his head. He was serious, even sad. All of a sudden I remembered the dream about my mom. She'd shaken her head at me, too, the same way. "If I ever saw you do something that wasn't ninety-percent selfish, I'd die of shock," Josh said.

It was a low blow. It stung. "Promises, promises," I said quickly.

I rounded Dionne's corner on two wheels, then slammed down on the brakes. She and Murray were outside. "De!" I hollered. Then I told Josh, "I'm going to hang, take the Jeep home."

" 'Josh, would you *please* take the Jeep home for me?' " he said.

I was halfway across De's front lawn. "What's the big deal, you have to go back anyway. No need to wig."

Josh waved to Dionne and Murray, then drove away.

"Josh is single, isn't he?" De asked, staring after the Jeep.

"Most likely," I said.

"Maybe we should fix him up with someone."

"No way! Don't make me hurl."

"Why not?" Dionne said. "He's cute."

Objectively, he was. Josh's dark hair was thick and unruly. He had dynamite baby blues, with a shag of dark brows not too different from my father's. And, of course, there were all those expensive white teeth. But to me, he was the same pain he'd always been. Still trying to tease me, teach me, rescue me, better me.

"I beg to differ," I told Dionne.

"I still think he's a Baldwin," she persisted.

"Whatever," I said, making the *W* sign. "Where are we going?"

We climbed into the BMW where De and Murray did their Ike and Tina routine on which place served the ultimate yogurt. De said Penguins. Murray was all Humphrey Yogurt.

"I don't care what you said. You say all you want," said De. "We're still going to Penguins. What do you say, Cher?"

"Penguins."

"Two against one. It's Penguins."

Murray started up the car while De and I broke into song—Queen Latifah's "U-N-I-T-Y." We were wiggling and poking our arms through the sunroof and singing at the top of our lungs.

"U-N-I-T-Y . . . You gotta let them know . . . where to get the yogurt . . ."

Murray was grumbling, "Penguins, they don't mix no fruit there. They got toppings, but toppings are whack. . . ."

The louder I sang, the easier it was to forget Josh and the Tree People and Marky Mark and all their terrific contributions.

Chapter 5

I pride myself on not dwelling on negativity, but I was bummed about being called selfish. A whole day later it was still on my mind. I talked to De about it at the school lunch court. Sort of.

It was a totally sunny day. Half the kids in the Quad were wearing shades to ward off the glare from the bright blue metal tables. I took off my Oliver Peoples. "De, would you call me selfish?"

"No way!" she insisted. "Well, not to your face."

"Really?"

Dionne laughed. "What's wrong? Is Josh snapping on you because he's going through his postadolescent idealistic phase?"

Just then I spotted Mr. Hall. "There he is," I

said, refocusing on the job at hand. "Come on." I grabbed my thermos, which was filled with coffee I'd bought on the way to school that morning. By the fluid ounce, the stuff was slightly more expensive than White Diamonds.

"Hi. Bold fashion statement," I said, genuinely admiring the denim shirt Hall was wearing under his trusty sweater vest. There was also a bow tie I'd never seen before, colorful yet not gaudy. "Mr. Hall, do you drink coffee?" I asked.

"Not from this cafeteria, but yes, under normal circumstances."

"Well, I'm such an idiot. When I packed Daddy's lunch this morning, I gave him my lemon Snapple and took this nasty Italian Roast." I opened the thermos and let the premium blend toy with his nostrils. "Would you like it?"

He breathed in the aroma. "Mmmm. Are you sure you don't want it?" Mr. Hall asked politely. His eyes were actually glistening. He looked like he'd chew my hand off at the wrist to get it.

"Duh!" I said. "It might stunt my growth, and I want to be five ten like Cindy Crawford. I figured either you or *Miss Geist* would enjoy it." Then I went for super-casual. "I mean, maybe you guys could share it."

We left him guarding the thermos and headed out to scout the Quad for Geist. "I've got a feeling we'll achieve contact today," I told De. Sure enough, Miss Geist was standing near the napkin dispensers, scrubbing mustard off her dress.

"Hi, Miss Geist," Dionne said.

"Oh, hello, girls. Did you sign up for the environmental fair yet?" she asked, sliding her glasses back up the bridge of her nose.

"That's a real pretty dress," I said to charge her confidence.

She was totally insecure. "Is it okay?"

"It's funky," De told her.

"But you've got to fix the hair," I said. "These clips are *so* eighties." Before she could object, I took them out and started fluffing her hair.

"Cher, please." She tried to duck.

"Wait, wait. Just let me make tendrils." I practically had to beg.

"Please, Miss Geist," Dionne urged. "It's really starting to look dope. Hang in there, I'll get that stain on your skirt."

We finished up and sent her on her way. "Remember to sign up for the fair," she called over her shoulder.

"Not a total Betty," De decided. "But a vast improvement."

"I did what I could. We'd better book if we're going to go to PE."

We started crossing the Quad. "I feel like bailing," Dionne said.

"I know what you mean, but at least it's exercise. I'm such a heifer. I had *two* bowls of Special K this morning."

"Cher, look!" De jerked my arm.

I turned and there they were, Miss Geist and Mr. Hall, leaning against a table, talking together. "Look at that smile. She looks so cute."

"Now we're talking photo op," De said.

We watched as Mr. Hall poured Miss Geist a cup of the coffee. He drank out of the thermos.

"Is that a tearjerker, or what?" De sighed.

"Look at the body language," I pointed out. "She's not slouching. He's not picking at his vest. They're facing each other! It's an unequivocal invite."

After a while, Mr. Hall took out his pen and wrote something down.

"Wow, look, he's getting her digits!" Dionne squeezed my arm.

"Aw, look at Geist."

"Adorable!"

"Yeah," I said, "old people can be so sweet!"

For the next week or so, I was totally golden. Mr. Hall, all cleaned and pressed, was handing back reports that had the whole class ecstatically wigging. Elton got a B plus on one paper and spun me around in the hall. Travis was practically in a coma after receiving his first-ever passing grade. Even Amber Salk congratulated me.

Dionne and I were on our cellulars hourly, trading sightings and updates. "He's walking her to her car," De would report. We'd rush out of class, meet at the Quad, and sneakily follow them. One afternoon we spotted them in Geist's car, talking. "Kiss her, kiss her," we cheered in whispers.

Awkwardly, Mr. Hall leaned over and gave Miss Geist a little peck good-bye. De and I shrieked and slapped a high five.

The next day, a Friday, Miss Geist erased an enormous assignment from her homework blackboard and wrote instead, "Have a great weekend." The class did a collective "Huh?!"

When I entered the lunch court at noon, I was greeted with applause, which I acknowledged with gracious modesty. I floated through the rest of the school day, receiving the winks, smiles, and gratitude of my peers, but I couldn't wait to see Daddy.

That afternoon I found him hard at work in his office at home. I brought him tea and cookies.

"What's this all about?" he asked, opening the envelope I'd stuck on top of his papers.

"My report card," I said.

He looked it over. "Is this still the same semester?"

"Uh-huh." I poured his tea.

"So what was the chain of events here?" he grumbled. "You handed in some extra-credit reports?"

"No."

"They let you take the midterms over?"

"Uh-uh."

"Are you saying you argued your way up from a C plus to an A minus?" he asked suspiciously.

"Totally based on my powers of persuasion," I confessed.

He came around the desk and hugged me. "That's my girl."

"Are you proud?"

"I couldn't be happier than if it was based on real grades." He smacked the report card with the back of his hand. "Now, this is the kind of accomplishment that tells me I won't have to worry about my little girl."

I took the report card into the living room. "So, Ma," I said, waving it at her portrait. "Solid gold. Now we just have to get Daddy's cholesterol count down."

Chapter 6

I was genuinely moved by the effects of romance on Miss Geist and Mr. Hall. They were dressing better, with consciousness if not furious flair. The only dent in my joy was Josh's rant about selfishness. But I could see what he meant about Marky Mark. I was feeling way magnanimous and wanted to do more good deeds.

I was musing on this during Ms. Stoeger's PE class. Dionne and I were standing in line under the blinding sun. We were supposed to be working on our tennis strokes. There was one automated machine hurling tennis balls, and about twelve girls waiting in front of us.

"Follow through, always follow through," Stoeger was shouting as the line inched forward.

Dionne had a sneezing fit and blew her nose. "Ow, ow, ow," she hollered, squirming in pain.

"De, when your allergies act up," I told her, "take out your nose ring."

By the time it was my turn to hit the ball, I had totally spaced.

"Earth to Cher!" Ms. Stoeger called rudely. "Come in, Cher."

"I just want to say that physical education here is a sham," I announced, taking the tennis racquet from Summer Bass, who'd just whacked two home runs over the fence. "Standing in line for forty minutes barely works off the calories in a stick of Care Free gum."

"But you've certainly exercised your mouth, Cher." Stoeger fought to be heard over the cheers of my classmates. "Now hit the ball."

This yellow ball came flying out of the machine. I swung at it and missed. Ooops, no Olympics for me.

"What have I been saying all day?" asked Stoeger.

"You've been saying, 'Next . . . next . . .'"

"I've been saying, *Follow through!*" She demonstrated. The insignia tattoo on her bicep pulsed impressively. "Follow through!"

"But I missed the ball already. Why should I continue something that didn't even occur?"

Another ball whizzed by, dangerously close to my head.

"And, Ms. Stoeger, that machine is just a lawsuit waiting to happen."

"Thanks for the legal advice," she barked. "Dionne, you're up."

"Ms. Stoeger," De said, "I have a note from my tennis instructor. He'd prefer if I didn't expose myself to any training that might derail his teachings."

Stoeger's nostrils flared in disgust. "Fine. Amber, your turn."

"Ms. Stoeger, my plastic surgeon doesn't want me doing any activity where balls fly at my nose," she announced.

"All right! Enough!" Stoeger hollered. I thought she was going to lose it. Just then Mr. Goodman, the principal, walked onto the court. Stoeger sucked in her gut and performed this amazing smile.

There was a kid with Mr. Goodman, a girl with huge doe eyes outlined in crude black pencil, and red and purple streaks in her too black hair. She was wearing a shapeless flannel shirt and baggy jeans that puddled around worn high-tops.

"Eeeyuw," Amber whispered behind us. "What's that?"

"Does the word 'schlub' ring a bell?" Alana Caplin asked.

"Ladies, we have a new student with us," the principal announced. "This is Tai Frazer."

We shouted in unison: "Hi, Tai!"

Shyly, the new girl shrugged her shoulders. "Ay, owsit goin?" she mumbled.

"What did she say?" everyone asked.

"I think it's New York for 'Hey, how is it going?'" Summer translated helpfully. Her father is a network anchor who covers war zones around the world, so she could speak a little New York.

Stoeger handed the kid a tennis racquet. "Tai, you won't have time to change, but you can hit a few balls in those clothes."

"She could be a farmer in those clothes," Amber said.

A few girls laughed. Tai kind of flinched. She gave this little hurt grin and shrugged her shoulders again. I have to say her innocence stirred me. And her baggy jeans reminded me of Marky Mark. It came to me all at once. Here was someone I could help. Here was someone brutally in need of just my kind of contribution.

"De, my mission is clear. Look at that girl." We were watching her together. She looked lost. She didn't know if she was supposed to hit the ball or wait in line. "She's so adorably clueless," I said, and waved Tai over. "De, we've got to adopt her."

"Cher, please. She's a tow-up. Our stock would plummet."

"But we should use our popularity for a good cause," I explained.

Dionne was still shaking her head when Tai came over, but I knew she'd given in.

"Ay," Tai greeted us.

"Hang with us," I said.

"Thanks."

"You're from New York?"

"Umbuh-lievable," she said. She was amazed. "How'd ya know?"

"How do you like California?" I asked.

"I'm freakin', man. I could use some herbal refreshment."

"We do lunch in ten minutes," Dionne said graciously. "They've got a great endive and arugula salad."

"I'd better see about a table," I said, pulling out my cellular phone and dialing the lunch court. "Hi, Brent . . . Yeah . . . Is our regular table available? Yeah. Well, there'll be an extra joining us. Okay. Peace."

After class De and I walked Tai over to the cafeteria and showed her around.

"That's Alana's group over there." I pointed them out. "They do the TV station, and they think that's the most important thing on earth. You like working on TV stations?"

"Not really," Tai said.

"Then forget them," De told her. "They just hang by themselves."

"There's the 'Persian Mafia.' You can't hang with them unless you own a BMW," I explained.

"Yeah, right," she said.

I showed her the guys, next. Murray, Elton, and their crowd were at their usual table out at the food court. "That's the Crew. The foremost men at our school."

"Including my boyfriend," Dionne added quickly. She blew Murray a kiss. "Ain't he cute?"

"*If* you make the decision to date a high school boy, those are the only acceptable ones," I told Tai.

"Which is your boyfriend?" she asked.

"As if!"

"Cher's got attitude about high school boys," De explained.

"It's a personal choice every woman has to make for herself," I said as Murray made his way toward us with a practiced hip-hop bounce.

"Woman, lend me five dollars," he called to Dionne.

"I have asked you repeatedly not to call me woman," she said.

Murray worked on glaring at her. "What's your problem? I don't see no narrow hips squeezed into your 501s, so I can't call you Man," he said.

"A mere generic reference to my sex is *not* an identity," De grumbled.

"Excuse me, 'Ms. De-ionne,' " said Murray. "But street slang is an increasingly valid form of expression. Most feminine pronouns have mocking, but not necessarily misogynistic, undertones." He turned his Beverly Hills High cap around, gave De a head wag, and left.

"Umbuh-lievable," said Tai. "You guys talk like grown-ups!"

"Well, this is a really good school," I told her.

"I guess," she said. "Ay, I'm gettin' a soda, you guys want?"

We steered Tai over to the beverage area and left her there. De and I got in the food line. "She's nice," Dionne admitted.

"Yes, and there's so much to be done with her." Affectionately, I watched Tai, notebook in hand, trying to negotiate the drink line. She had forgotten to pick up a glass, then realized it, and was now back at the end of the line. I waved to her. She caught my eye and shrugged shyly.

"The clothes are totally 1992," I said. "And what do you call that hair color? But there is definitely hottie potential. I'm feeling way inspired."

"You go, girl," De said.

Skateboard under his arm, Travis had just sneaked into line behind Tai. He glanced over her shoulder and broke into a big grin. Tai sensed him looking at her and turned.

"Nice representation," Travis said, nodding at the surrealistic cartoons covering the front of her notebook.

"Thanks," she said, then nodded at his skateboard. "Umbuh-lievable stickers."

That was all I heard. De and I got involved in a lettuce discussion, about which had fewer calories, endive, arugula, or basic bib. Then we got our food and were putting it out on the table when Tai returned.

"I met this umbuh-lievable guy," she said. "Long hair, funny . . ."

"Skateboard?" I asked.

"Yeah! How'd'ya know?" She was radically impressed. "He showed me his board, and he was saying that he thought it was getting too cluttered, so I told him I like the stickers, but he wanted to clear this entire area out and concentrate on one decorative statement . . . maybe Marvin the Martian, he said. I said, 'Get out of town! I can do Marvin the Martian! I mean there's not much to him, but,' I said, 'Look,' and I showed him my notebook where I draw all these Marvin cartoons."

She spotted Travis carrying his lunch tray, and waved. "There he is!"

Travis started to wave back, then realized he was holding the tray and went into this farcical struggle to get it balanced.

De and I exchanged looks.

"Tai, how old are you?" I asked her.

"I'll be sixteen in May."

"My birthday's in April. As someone who's older, can I give you some advice?" I wanted to be delicate about this. But Travis was a bonehead. He hung with these baked-out boardees, whose idea of a good time was doubling their daily dose of Prozac. "Tai, I don't want to sound all judgmental and all, but it's one thing to have a friend who's . . . well, funny. And it's quite another to have one who's totally fried."

"You see the distinction?" De asked.

"Yeah . . ." Tai said tentatively.

"The boardees generally hang in the stairwell

over there." I pointed out a smoky area peopled by collapsed students whose mouths moved as they tried to sound out the words of the comic books they were flipping through.

"Sometimes they get to class and say bonehead things, and we all laugh of course. But no respectable girl actually dates them. I don't mean to be harsh, but you don't want to start off on the wrong foot, do you?"

"Do you have a dependency problem?" Dionne asked delicately. "Because they have groups here."

"I don't think so," Tai said.

She looked dazed and confused. "Hey, I've got a great idea!" I said to cheer her. "Let's do a makeover."

"Whaddya mean?"

"Do your makeup, figure your colors, replan your wardrobe . . ."

"Noo . . ." Tai began.

"Ah, let her," De said. "Cher's main thrill in life is makeovers. It gives her a sense of control in a world of chaos."

"Pleeease," I said.

"Well, yeah . . . sure. Gee, you guys!" Tai said emotionally, "I've never had like *friends* before."

She'd never been to a house like mine before, either. She was awed and floored by it—literally. Staring up at the domed ceiling of the entrance hall, she tripped and tumbled down into the living room. Dionne rolled her eyes.

Tai dusted herself off. "Umbuh-lievable, who thought of making curtains like that?" she asked, checking out the window treatments. "Lookit that chandelier! You guys must be rich!"

"Come on, Tai. We've got a lot of work to do." I took her arm and dragged her along.

"Really, really a lot," De said, following us up the stairs.

Tai began to tremble as I pressed the button that opened the automated doors of my walk-in closet. "It's like a garage," she breathed as the mirrored doors slid back. "It's like a department store," she whispered, staring at the color-coordinated racks. "It's like . . . K Mart in the Bronx!" I flipped the switch to start the clothes rack rotating. "Umbuh-lievable," Tai gasped.

Dionne flicked on the dressing table lights and sat Tai down before the mirror. De broke out the makeup. I chose three hairbrushes, two round and a regular, and tucked the blow dryer into my belt. The transformation was about to begin.

An hour later we had cut the bottom off Tai's shirt, pulled her hands away from her stomach, and twirled her in front of the full-length three-way mirror.

Tai stared at herself. Her mouth fell open. Her eyes misted over. "Uhm-believable, I look just like you!" she gasped gratefully. She hugged us, and we all jumped up and down screaming.

"Okay, now let's work out." We shimmied into these classic neon spandex togs, and De and I led Tai to the den. I popped *Buns of Steel* into the VCR. You know that famous expression, Teacher, heal thyself? Well, it's true. As we got into molding Tai, I found myself on quite a self-improvement kick.

Fifteen minutes into *Buns,* Tai collapsed onto her mat. "I can't do another lift. I'll never move again. Ever."

"It'll get easier," De promised, "as long as we do it every day, not just sporadically."

"How do you know if you're doing it sporadically?" Tai asked.

"That's another thing, Tai," I explained as gently as I could. I really didn't want to hurt her feelings. "We've got to work on your accent and vocabulary. Like *sporadic* means once in a while. Try to use it in a sentence today, and find some other expression besides *unbelievable,* okay?"

Tai nodded earnestly. I dragged her over to the pile of books I'd set out on the coffee table. "Okay, from now on we're alternating Cindy Crawford's *Aerobicize* and *Buns of Steel* and reading one nonschool book a week. My first book is *Fat to Fit."*

Tai looked through the books. "Mine is *Men Are from Mars, Women Are from Venus,"* she said.

"That takes care of our minds and bodies. We should also do something cool for mankind or the planet a couple of hours."

De cocked her head at me, like "what did you have in mind?"

Someone coughed and we all jumped. Torn

between curiosity and amusement, Josh was staring at us from the door of the den. There was this vague smile on his face, as if he didn't know exactly what we were up to, but he thought the possibilities might be entertaining.

"How long have you been here?" I demanded.

Josh shrugged. "Hey, what's going on?"

"Ugh . . . the dreaded Ex," I said to Tai. "Tai, this is Josh. Josh, Tai."

"Ay," said Tai.

"Nice to meet you," Josh replied. "What're you guys doing?"

"Something you should give immediate and serious thought to—self-improvement. Hey, you know about this stuff," I said. "I want to do something good for humanity."

"Promise you'll never have children," said Josh, turning and walking out.

De and Tai laughed. "Excuse me," I told them, and followed Josh into the kitchen. "So what do you *truly* think?" I said.

"I'm amazed."

"That I'm devoting myself so generously to someone else?"

"No, that you found someone even more clueless than you are to worship you."

His words stung, but I chose not to dwell on Josh's negativity. "I'm rescuing her from a lonely teenage limbo. You know, the wounds of adolescence can take years to heal."

"And you've never had a mother, so you're

acting out on that poor girl as if she was your Barbie doll."

"Oh, grow up, Josh. You always say that. You always drag my mom into it." It was true, of course, but something was brutally wrong. Josh's barbs were actually hitting the mark. I was feeling wounded instead of angry. I struck back as best I could. "Freshman psych rears its ugly head," I said sarcastically.

"I'm not taking psych."

"What*ever*. I am going to take that lost soul in there and make her well dressed and popular. Her life will be better because of me. How many girls say that about you?"

I left the kitchen. Josh followed me. De and Tai were watching TV in the den, mindlessly singing along with a commercial. Josh waved at them from the door.

"Bye," Tai said.

"Be seeing you," said Josh.

"I hope not sporadically," Tai called, and beamed at me proudly.

Chapter 7

Our work was paying off. As De, Tai, and I crossed the Quad, I couldn't help noticing how many guys smiled at Tai. I whispered to De, "Do you see how boys are responding? My heart is totally bursting."

"I know," Dionne said. "I'm kvelling."

It was an outstanding morning. The sun was bright, throwing palm tree shadows across the Quad. There was barely enough crud in the air to justify the A.M. smog alert. The school courtyard reverbed with nature's sounds: the chirping of birds, the chatter of kids on their cellulars, the beeping of car locks . . . what*ever*.

"Ay, there's Travis," Tai said.

I was distressed to see how her face lit up at the sight of him. He was standing outside the cafeteria, holding up a cardboard sign. He looked like one of those airport chauffeurs. Only instead of looking for someone who'd ordered a limo, Travis was trolling for homework. Mr. Diemer's Colony Homework. That's what it said on his sign.

"Do you have Diemer's homework?" he was asking passing groups of kids as we approached. "Stuff about the thirteen colonies? Tenth-grade history? Hey, Cher, are you in Diemer's class?"

"Geist," I told him.

"Tai!" Travis beamed. He actually and suddenly looked alert. It was like haul out the camcorder and capture this for *Hard Copy: Coma Boy Wakes!* "Hey, you guys get this yet?" Travis handed us a couple of xeroxed flyers, and we kept walking.

"Wow," Tai said. "A party!"

"Yeah, but it's in the Valley," I said. "The police usually shut them down in less than an hour, and it takes almost that long to get there."

"Besides, it's just locals," De added. "And you don't want to be seen in the Valley."

"Nah," Tai said, but she looked like she thought it would be fun. "You think Travis is going?"

"Tai, I thought we had moved on from there," I said.

"Don't download yourself now," De said. "You've got something going for you that hardly anyone else at school does."

"Yeah, mystery," I told her. "Tai, as far as

everyone's concerned, you were the most popular girl in your school. Everyone's curious, and the fact that you hang with De and me . . ."

"Speaks very highly of you," De said, finishing the thought. "You have to take advantage of this window of opportunity."

"That's right. If you strike while the iron is hot, you could have any guy you want."

"Like who?" Tai asked.

"Let's see . . . who's available? Brandon, Bronson . . . Oh, I got it! Elton's single now. He just broke up with Valette."

"Who's Elton?"

"He was in debate with us. He did the 'in favor of animal testing' speech."

Tai looked disappointed. "Oh," she said. "The guy with the huge ID bracelet that says ELTON?"

"He's way popular," Dionne assured her. "He's like the social director of the crew."

"Plus his dad can get you into *any* concert. And, I noticed him scoping you out."

"Really?" Tai said. "He was looking at me?"

"Tscha! He said you gave him a toothache," I continued.

"How'd I do that?"

"It's an expression. It means he thinks you're sweet."

Tai stopped and stared at me. "Yeah?" she said, interested now. "Wow."

Behind Tai's back, Dionne silently mouthed the words: Is that true?

I rolled my eyes. Of course it wasn't. But it was

an excellent idea. Nothing would set Tai's self-esteem and stock soaring like hooking up with one of the Crew's major hotties. And Elton, with his brutally now taste in clothing and CDs, was a matchless catch.

Could I make it happen? Could a 6.7 quake level the LA Freeway? I could hardly concentrate in school, except to note that there was a jelly jar full of spring flowers on Miss Geist's desk and a radical new aftershave wafting off Mr. Hall. Then, in PE, Amber Salk showed me this picture of herself with a new nose, high cheekbones, and chin padding. It was a computer photograph that she'd had done at this cosmetic imaging center, but it was way inspiring. I don't mean the way Amber looked in the picture—which was like seeing a hamburger patty trying to turn into a sirloin steak—but the photo idea.

Right after Stoeger's class, I hurried to the photography lab and, with a minimum of wheedling, borrowed a camera. I got hold of Elton and some other guys from the Crew, and then I snagged Tai and De.

"It's a project," I told everyone as I posed them. "It's about friendship." Elton was front and center. Tai was standing in the back row. Actually, she was *behind* the back row. "Tai, I can't see you," I called. "Get in front." I pointed to the spot next to Elton, but Tai wound up next to Summer.

"Wait. Go girl, boy, girl, boy," I instructed. They stumbled around. "Come on, you guys, closer . . . Elton, put your arm around Tai." He did. Tai was beaming. I took the picture. "Great . . . oooh, Tai, come over here." This time I moved Tai around for a portrait. I got her standing so that the sun was behind her. It made her hair look soft and shiny. She was all framed with glowing leaves. She looked like an acne ad.

"Cool picture," Elton said.

I worked my way around Tai, and got pictures of her from every angle. "Doesn't she look classic?" I asked, tilting Tai's head professionally.

"This is beautiful," Elton said to Tai. "You're going to love this."

"Doesn't she look like one of those Botticelli chicks?" I said, encouraging him. Tai smiled.

"Would you make an extra print for me?" Elton asked.

Totally cool, I said, "Sure."

"What are you doing tonight?" I asked Tai on the way home from school. It was about a week after the photo session. "Want to have dinner at my house?"

"Do we have to work out? I'm kind of wiped."

"We'll take a break and just celebrate your popularity, okay?"

That renewed her.

We listened to CDs and did homework for a while. The dining table was all set up, but Lucy was nowhere in sight. Tai and I went in and sat down. Then Daddy came in. "Hi, this is my new friend, Tai," I said, introducing them.

He looked at her. "Get out of my chair," he said.

Tai moved. Dad sat down. Lucy appeared. She brought out a dish and ran away. "Thanks, Luce," I called after her. "It looks great."

"What is this garbage?" Daddy said.

"Dad, it's from the *Cut Your Cholesterol* cookbook. Dr. Lovett says you've got to get down to two hundred." My beeper went off. I checked, it was Dionne. "Uh-oh," I said, "this might be important."

"No calls at the table," Daddy announced. "We're going to have a nice family dinner."

After that no one said anything. In the kitchen, even Lucy's shoes stopped squeaking. You could hear the lawn sprinklers hissing, but that was about it. Finally, Daddy said, "What did you do in school today?"

I thought about it. "Well . . ." I volunteered. "I broke in my purple clogs."

Daddy's phone rang. He picked it up, of course, and started going through depositions with a client. While he was busy, I sneakily dialed Dionne. "What's up?" I whispered.

"Okay. So Murray's geometry class is right by Elton's locker, and Elton was getting his books, and taped up inside was the picture you took of Tai."

"No!" I squealed.

"T.b.," Dionne assured me.

"Tai," I whispered across the table. "Elton's got your picture hanging in his locker."

"Umbuh-lievable!" Tai said.

"Anyway, most of the Crew will be appearing at this Val party, Cher," Dionne continued. "Now what do we do?"

"Ordinarily, I would never . . . but as a friend to Tai, it's our duty to go," I told De, then I broke it to Tai. "Looks like we'll have to do a cameo in the Valley."

"Yes!" she said.

Chapter 8

The night arrived. I lent Tai a totally classic little fawn-colored suede number, which brought out the Bambi in her eyes. For myself I chose a hot red Alaïa with a ruffle of festive black faux feathers. Murray picked us up. De was riding shotgun, poring through a Thomas guide. No one knew exactly where the Valley was.

"What are you looking at? Sun Valley is north. Look at the top of the map," Murray instructed.

"All I see is Bel Air," De said.

"Turn the page. Follow the Hollywood Freeway."

"Is that the red line?" De asked.

Murray grabbed the map from her while I prepped Tai. "Act like you don't notice Elton until he comes up to you," I suggested. "Then smile at him, but make sure it looks like you were having fun anyway."

"Okay. So I like don't notice him, then I do, and I'm all like smiling, but I'm also all smiling before I like see him? . . . I don't get it," Tai said.

By the time we hit the Val, we agreed that I'd stay close and feed her the strategy a little at a time.

When we finally arrived, the party house was blazing with lights and music. The driveway, lawn, and most of the street was crammed with cars, many of them reputable European brands. There were a few troubling exceptions—big wheels, pickups, an ancient VW with customized flames, and a couple of dirt bikes.

The local guests primarily wore hugely baggy pants and shirts. Blending right in, Travis whizzed by on his skateboard and gave Tai and me a welcoming shove in passing.

"Hey!" I snapped. Tai laughed. "Skateboards," I told her regaining my composure. "That is *so* three years ago!"

Then Travis did a total major flip off a banister. "Wow!" Tai said. "Dja see that?"

Dionne and Murray were barely through the door before they started dancing. "Ragin'," Tai said, taking in the action.

I studied the crowd, the furnishings, the music, the options. "Let's do a lap before we commit to a location," I suggested.

We excused and elbowed our way along. Behind us, Murray and Dionne started arguing.

"Hey." Tai tugged at my sleeve and pointed to Amber, who was jostling through the crush. "Ain't that the same dress as yours?"

"What a clone!" I raged. I brushed by her. "Say, Ambular, was that *you* going through my laundry?"

"As if!" scoffed the red-clad empress of split ends. "Like I would wear something from Judy's."

"I'd call you a fashion victim, but I understand you people prefer 'ensembly challenged.'"

Travis came over and spilled his drink. I tried to hop out of the way. It didn't work. "Great!" I sighed. "Ruin my red suede shoes, why don't you?" I grabbed a nearby napkin and started blotting the puddle on my instep.

Tai smiled at Travis. "Oh, I'm sorry," he said to her instead of me.

I went into the kitchen to get some paper towels for the shoe. "This is *so* not fixable," I said.

Tai and Travis had trailed me in. "A small price to pay to the party gods," he said.

Near the kitchen entrance, Elton was complaining loudly about the music selection. "E.M.F.? What is this, a time warp?" He started sorting through the CDs, searching for acceptable sounds.

"Elton's over there," I whispered to Tai. "Okay, act like Travis is saying something funny."

Tai looked at Travis, then got practically hysterical. Travis grinned, grateful to have gotten a laugh, but you could see he was struggling to remember how. Finally, he gave up thinking and just laughed along. A minute later, though, he whispered to Tai, "What's so funny?"

"Nothing," she told him.

Now he was really confused. Elton walked into the kitchen. "That's more like it," he said about the music.

Summer showed up at the door. "Come on, let's play suck and blow."

Tai's eyes sparked. "What was that?"

"Come on," Elton said. "It'll pass the time."

"You play it with a credit card," I explained to Tai as we headed for the den. "Everyone sits close together. One person sucks in the credit card and passes it to the next person by blowing while the other sucks. Like ATM machines with lips."

Elton pulled us into the circle. Tai was on one side of him, I was on the other. But when he had to pass the card to me, he dropped it and our lips touched. This was not going the way I'd planned. Luckily, Dionne started screaming.

We dashed out into the hall. The noise was coming from upstairs. Dionne and Murray were yelling at each other while other party goers looked on. Murray's head was covered with shaving cream, like a giant foamy mushroom hat. "Look at this!" De shouted to me and Tai. "Look what that fool's doing."

"It's going to look good," Murray insisted.

"Look at Lawrence." He grabbed his friend's bald head to demonstrate.

"Eeeuuuw!" De went ballistic.

"That's harsh," said Lawrence.

"I think you look good," Murray consoled his friend.

"As will you," Lawrence said.

"What do you care what *he* thinks? I'm the one who has to look at you." It was just like at school. Only now it was all the party goers who were joining in the discussion, taking sides. "And right before the yearbook pictures," De said to me. "What will I tell people when they say, 'Who was your boyfriend?' What will I say to my grandchildren?"

She started dialing her cellular phone. "I'm going to tell your mother. Let's see what she thinks."

Murray's eyes went frantic. He grabbed for the phone. "Don't you be doing that."

"I'm doing it," De said.

They wrestled over the phone. De managed to get into the bathroom and slam the door. Murray pounded on it. The divided crowd rooted for its favorites. "Same thing happened at the spring dance," I told Tai, steering her downstairs. "De spent the entire 'after' party in the bathroom. Come on, let's go bump into people."

"I'm cool with that," Tai said.

We started to dance. Travis decided to try moshing, ages after the trend. He dove down onto the crowd, knocking people over and fostering attitude. He was greeted with shoves and bumps and a roar of "Watch it! Whaddya postal? You're toast!" and "Cut it out!"

Tai came to his rescue. "Are you okay?" she asked, helping him up.

"Boy, where's your sense of pit hospitality?" Travis shouted at the dancers as he limped to the sidelines.

He gave Tai a what-do-you-expect look. "Sun Valley," he explained, shaking his limp blond hair out of his eyes.

"That was so cool," she said. "I wish I could do that."

"No, don't!" Travis cautioned.

"Why not?"

"If girls did it, what could guys do to impress them?"

"I dunno," Tai said coquettishly. "Stuff."

They were flirting! I hurried over. "Tai, I need you," I said, dragging her away. We'd worked so hard together. She looked great. Her schoolwork was improving. And Travis was such a burned-out Barney. She deserved better. "Elton's right over there. Pull out some of your New York street moves."

We waded into the sound. Tai was impressive, moving like a music video goddess. An equally devoted dancer across the room did an energetic kick. One of her clogs went flying off and hit Tai on the head. Tai crumpled like a Kleenex. I screamed, "Tai! Tai! Elton, help me."

We carried her to the kitchen. I put ice in a

towel and gave it to Elton to hold on Tai's head. Travis showed up a minute later. He looked dangerously worried. He wanted to be helpful. He was holding a handful of dripping ice cubes for Tai. "You should use ice," he said.

"Travis, we've got it covered," I assured him.

He knelt down next to Tai. "Are you okay?" he whispered, all concerned.

I pulled him up and eased him out. "Tai would want you to enjoy the party," I said. "If it's a concussion," I told Elton, "you have to make sure she stays conscious. Ask her questions."

Elton said, "Tai! Tai! What's seven times seven?"

"No, ask her stuff she knows."

Tai's eyelids fluttered. "Owww," she groaned, and sat up.

"That's some bump you've got there," Elton said.

"I'm all right."

"Think you can go back out there?" he asked encouragingly.

Tai nodded.

"Okay, let's see. Can you do this?" He started moving to the music. "Slide, slide, slippity slide . . ." Elton was swinging his arms in the air like they did in the video. Tai started doing it, too. They did it together and laughed. It was way heartwarming. "Come on," Elton said. Taking Tai by the hand, he led her back to the dance floor.

Chapter 9

I slipped out to the backyard. It was a warm, perfect night. There was hardly any humidity. You could totally count on your hair not frizzing. There was lots of making out going on around and in the pool. I took off my shoes and sat down with my feet in the water. Love was everywhere. And even though I was alone, I was so happy for Tai. I remembered that long book they'd made us read that said, "Tis a far, far better thing," like when you do stuff for other people.

My reverie was harshly interrupted when a boy rushed over to puke in the pool. Swimmers started screaming and jumping out. Just then my beeper went off. I checked the number, then dug out my cellular and phoned home.

Daddy's voice crackled through the chaos at the pool. "Do you know what time it is?"

"A watch doesn't really go with this outfit," I said.

"Where are you?"

What was I going to say, the Valley? It was only hours from home and light-years from civilization through some seriously depressed real estate. And there was Daddy's cholesterol to consider. "I'm just having a snack with my girlfriends," I said.

Just then a helicopter flew over the house.

"Where? In Rwanda?" he demanded.

"Is that in the Valley?"

I could tell his count was climbing. "I expect you to walk through the door in twenty minutes!"

"Eew . . . it might take a little more than twenty minutes."

"Everywhere in LA takes twenty minutes," he stormed, and hung up.

I thought it through quickly and decided it was time to go.

Tai, Elton, and I walked to his car, a cute Porsche convertible. "Thanks for offering us a ride," I was saying. "Dionne and Murray are still milking their scene."

"My pleasure." Elton's normally slicked-back hair was all unruly. There were faint party fumes coming off his clothes.

Our friend Summer came over. "Pretty random fiesta."

"Big time," I said.

"You need a ride?" Summer asked.

"That'd be great!"

"I've got her," Elton said quickly.

"I'm right below Wilshire on Lindon," Summer reminded him.

"Hey, that's near me," Tai said.

I gave her a look, trying to remind her the idea was for *her* to leave with Elton. He was holding open the Porsche door. I tried to maneuver Tai toward it. But she was pretty unfocused. "I'm right above Olympic," she told Summer.

"Then you go with Summer," Elton said, "and I'll take Cher back. Cher, you're off Benedict, right?"

"Actually, you could take Wilshire to Canon, and that turns into Benedict." I was getting frantic, torn between trying to get Tai and Elton organized and trying to get home before the EMS came for Daddy.

"Then she'd have to go back south, and I'm already going north," Elton pointed out.

"But you could take Tai and drop her off on your way up to Sunset."

He took my arm and got me settled into the Porsche. "But—" I began. But Elton had climbed into the driver's seat. Suddenly, everyone was saying good-bye, and we were pulling out into the night, all in the wrong cars.

Elton's first concern was finding correct music.

What a surprise. He kept pumping CDs into the player and rejecting them after the merest snip of sound. It was giving me a headache, like those late-night TV music ads where the names of a thousand songs you never heard of roll by as catchy snatches of classics play in the background. But it gave me a chance to restructure my campaign. Tai might be out of sight, I decided, but I could definitely keep her in Elton's mind.

"Didn't Tai look cute tonight?"

"How about some Morrissey?" he asked, humming along with the doomed CD.

"I love how she looks with her hair up, you know. Like with curly tendrils hanging. But it's also so pretty when it's all wild. Like in that picture I took."

"You're an awesome photographer," Elton said.

This wasn't going the way I planned. "Well, when your subject is so attractive—"

"It's like you're using sunshine to paint a picture. Usually girls that are beautiful and popular don't bother developing any talents."

"I think, actually, I like Tai's hair down," I said.

"You know, I consider you one of my best friends, and I don't have friends that are girls."

"I'm really glad, because your happiness means a lot to me." That's why I think Tai would be so perfect for you, I was getting ready to say.

"It does?" Elton seemed encouraged.

"Sure. I mean, I saw how hard your breakup with Valette was."

"I think we both know what it's like to be lonely."

"What*ever,*" I said. "The thing is, I'd like to see you settled already."

Suddenly Elton pulled into a store's empty parking lot. We were in this definitely low-rent district. The store was shuttered with metal gates and rusty padlocks. "Hey, where are you going?" I asked.

Elton stopped the car and pounced on me. "I knew it, I knew it," he started saying.

I pushed him away. "You knew what?"

"That you were totally sprung on me." He grabbed my hand and started kissing it.

I snatched it away. "Hello! Don't you mean Tai?"

Elton reared back. "Tai?" he asked, totally shocked.

"Weren't you just dancing with her?"

"Yeah, I knew you wanted me to. I did you a props."

"You have her picture in your locker . . ." I was starting to get that sinking feeling. "Excuse me. I'm having a Twin Peaks experience," I told Elton.

He started kissing me again. I moved away. The door handle jammed into my spine, possibly damaging my jacket. I was trying not to panic.

"I felt it when you kissed me tonight," Elton said.

"I did *not* kiss you. Suck and blow is a *game!*"

He totally did not get it.

"Stop!" I shoved him away.

"What's the deal? You've been flirting with me all year."

Was there a tragic genetic flaw in Elton's gray matter? "As if! I've been trying to help you and Tai get together."

"What a burn. Why would *I* go with Tai?"

"Why not?"

"Why not? Why not!" Elton roared. "Do you even *know* who my father is?"

I felt like ralphing. "You are a snob and a half," I said, disgusted.

"Come on, Cher. Me and Tai makes no sense. You and me"—he came at me again—"that makes sense."

"Cut it out!"

"Come on," he whined.

"Stop it!" I shouted. Finally, I got a grip on the door handle, got out of the Porsche, and slammed the door shut.

"Cher, get back in the car," Elton said.

"Leave me alone," I yelled. He started the car and screeched away.

"Hey," I called at the retreating taillights. "Where are you going?!" I hadn't realized how dark the lot was until the car was gone. "Wow!" was all I could say as I picked my way toward the street through the trash-strewn gravel. Under a greenish streetlight I dialed information. "Can I have the number of a cab company?" I asked. "I don't know which one. What do you have out there?"

"Hand it over," a voice said.

I glanced over my shoulder. There was a gun pointed at me. A gun? I screamed. A teenage psycho in a hooded sweatshirt he had probably lifted from Wal-Mart was pointing a gun at me. "Give me the phone," he said.

I handed it to him. I was still working on the gun. I could hardly tear my eyes off it. The whole thing was way beyond dramatic. My heart was in full, furious cardiac alert.

"And the bag."

I handed it over.

"Now get down on the ground, facedown."

That did it. "But this is an Alaïa!" I cried.

"Get down!" He'd probably never heard of Alaïa. I should've known from that sweatshirt. My beeper went off. "What's that?" he growled.

"My beeper."

"Gimme," he said.

"Aw, come on. What good is it? You want my dad paging you?"

"You're starting to annoy me," he said. "And I'm the one with a gun. So give it here and get down."

I didn't see any alternative. I gave him the beeper and got down, and he ran away. Two whole seconds it took. There'd really been no reason for me to go prone on the parking lot gravel. It was such a sadistic touch. I got up. The evening had turned into a royal mess. Robbed, lost, and in dry-cleaning distress, I wandered a couple of blocks looking for a phone booth.

I didn't know the number of the party house, so I couldn't reach my friends. Daddy would kill me if he knew where I was. No money for a cab. There was only one person left to call . . . and I really, really didn't want to ask him for help. But my options had dwindled.

Chapter 10

I dialed the number of Josh's Westwood "pad." I could picture the scene at his end of the phone. Laundry and radical decor. Political posters, tons of books, outdated music.

"Hello," he said.

"Josh? You busy?" I gave him the benefit of the doubt. Also, I was crying, so the less I said, the better.

"Where are you?"

"You sound just like Daddy."

"Don't tell me you're calling to say hi."

"Who is it?" a girl's voice called in the background.

"It's Mel's daughter," Josh told her.

If an "oh" could sound annoyed, hers did.

Who was this person in Josh's room? Had

super-sib finally outgrown his awkward adolescence and become romantically abled? And why was I feeling so shriveled about it?

I took a deep breath and blurted out my story. "Okay, so I was at this party, and my designated driver tried to attack me. So I got out so he'd stop, but he drove off and deserted me, and a guy with a gun held me up and got my money and my phone and yelled at me, and forced me to ruin my dress—"

Josh cut me off. "Okay, okay. Where are you?"

"At a phone booth."

"That's helpful. You should be easy to find."

I squinted at the street signs. "Oh! I'm on Troost and Saticoy."

"Where is *that?*"

"Sun Valley," I said, super-casually.

"Great," Josh said. "Man, you owe me."

I held onto the phone for a couple of minutes after Josh hung up. I knew that once I replaced the receiver, I'd be totally alone again. Except for a dim light above the street signs, the neighborhood was brutally deserted. I wasn't sure whether it was better to stand under the light or cringe in the shadows. Finally, I said very loudly to the dial tone, "Oh, and listen, Josh, I'm running a little low on *bullets*. You know, for my *gun*—the one I *always* carry. Do you think you could bring me some?" Then I hung up.

The street was dark and dead quiet. The stores behind me were shuttered. No cars passed. No light shone through the scrappy shrubs and skinny trees across the way. They couldn't even afford crickets in that neighborhood. I was seriously alone—which I hate!

Some people whistle when they're afraid. Some people pray. As I paced back and forth in front of the phone, I did what I do under stress, I thought about shopping.

It's not as bad as it used to be. I used to be totally terrified about being left alone. Daddy says for years after Mom died, I'd practically go postal when he walked out of a room. He says at night, I used to sneak into his room and try to hide in the closet just so I wouldn't have to be by myself.

Embarrassingly pathetic. I barely remember it.

But I know that some of Mom's stuff was still in the closet back then. And that I'd curl up in this tent of tasteful silks and velvets and inhale the scent of Chanel that still clung to her clothes. The thought of her alive and shopping made me feel better.

It still works sometimes. To my surprise, so did the thought of Josh rushing to my rescue.

When Josh and his mother moved into our house, everything changed. Suddenly there were all these people and noise and Gail slamming in and out of doors and my dad laughing and crazy family dinners and phones ringing and Josh's friends teasing my friends and cannonballing into the pool and me and Josh arguing. He was always trying to help me do things I thought I could do by myself. It was like if I tripped, Josh would be there to catch me. If I fell, he'd rush over to pick me up.

After Josh came, I was never alone. Now, it seemed, neither was he.

He showed up with a Heather. She looked like one, too. Poetically long hair. Ankle-length floral skirt. Blocky boots. Tight black T. *Please.* They invited me into the backseat of the car, where I got to listen to their stimulating front-seat discussion. It was perfect for showing high school dropouts what they *weren't* missing in college.

"I suppose there's some merit in learning form straight off," Josh was saying.

Heather disagreed. "But he's taking our minds at their most fecund point and restraining them before they've wandered through the garden of ideas."

Getting mugged was one thing. Having to listen to this was something else. Given my choice, I'd have preferred choking on a fur ball.

"It's like Hamlet says, 'To thine own self be true,'" said the over-vocabularied Heather.

"Hamlet didn't say that," I told her.

"I think I remember *Hamlet* accurately," she announced.

"Well, I remember Mel Gibson accurately. And he didn't say it. That Polonius guy did."

Josh laughed. Heather tossed her head, sending a ripple of annoyance through her golden tresses. I was not sorry to see her go. Josh dropped her at her dorm. "I'm walking Heather to her door," he announced. "Try to stay out of trouble." I watched them stroll together. At the door to the dorm, Josh treated her to a kiss. I couldn't see if it was a lip or cheek job.

"Thanks a lot, Cher," he said, getting back in the car. "That was a real fun night."

"I can't believe after all I've been through, you insist on tormenting me," I complained. "I mean, hello, I had a gun pointed at my head. So you yell at me, and Elton abandons me, and now as soon as I get through the door, Daddy'll start screaming. Nobody cares about me."

"Okay, okay, I'm sorry. Calm down. You want to sit up front?" I climbed up to the seat next to him. "What happened with this Elton guy?" he asked.

All of a sudden, I felt like crying. It really surprised me. "He tried to sexually harass me," I blurted.

"And you did nothing to lead him on?"

"As if! I was only being seminice to get him together with Tai."

"So Tai likes him?"

"She does now," I said. "But if it wasn't for me, she'd say Travis."

Josh shook his head. "Cher, sometimes when people say things, they're trying to tell you something."

What was this? Josh imparting brotherly wisdom once more? I was overwhelmed. I just didn't feel up to dealing with it right then.

"Whoa," I said, like it was way too deep for me. "I have to think about that."

"When have you even had a boyfriend? What do you know?" he persisted.

"I know that Heather girl is all wrong for you," I said.

"Based on a half-hour acquaintance?"

"She's a downer and you're a downer. Two wrongs don't make a right."

Tscha! I saw him blink. He wanted to argue, but he knew I was onto something.

"Oh, really."

"You need an upper to balance you," I explained. "You plod, you need someone who skips. You're earthbound, you need someone to twinkle around you."

"Oh, really?" he said sarcastically. But he was checking me out, trying to decide how seriously I should be taken. You could see he wasn't all that comfortable trading places. What, Cher knowing something Super-Josh didn't?

Finally, he laughed. "Someone like you, for instance?" he said.

"As if!"

All day Sunday I worried about what I was going to say to Tai. The more I thought about it, the more I started to doubt myself, which I really hate. Even Fabianne, my masseuse, said I was holding a lot of tension.

Lucky for me there was some sort of pressure inversion causing the smog to build up so much that school was closed for two days. So I had time to prepare for the unpleasant task.

Tai wasn't that crazy about Elton anyway, I told myself. So the fact that he'd turned out to be misguided and a slime shouldn't really rock her. In fact, I'd never worked harder trying to get two people together. Even Travis had seemed more attractive to her. By Wednesday, when school reopened, I felt certain that Tai would accept reality with one of her endearing shrugs, and we could move on from there.

De and I caught up with her in PE. We were in the locker room, changing out of our gym clothes, when I casually broke the news.

Tai burst into tears. "It's my hips, isn't it?" she wailed.

Dionne and I protested loudly. "No, of course not, don't be stupid."

"You could do so much better," I said with total sincerity.

"He thinks he's all that." Dionne sniffed the air and snapped her fingers.

"Yeah, God's gift."

"You're too good for him," De said.

Tai was inconsolable. "If I'm too good for him, how come I'm not with him?" she asked, breaking into a new round of heartrending sobs.

I saw Tai's tears ruining her mascara. I saw them splashing in big black plops all over the cute shirt she'd just put on. Her nose, so natural and unique, was all red and runny. I felt like crying, too.

And then I thought of Josh. He'd be laughing at how bad I felt. He'd be lecturing me on selfishness and meddling and not listening to what other people say.

How had trying to help a less fortunate friend resulted in such a miseryfest?

I'm not big on wallowing. I hate living in the past. So I put a big, bright smile on my face, and lifted Tai's quivering chin. "I've got an idea. Let's blow off seventh and eighth, and go to the mall," I said. "We can walk around, see the new Christian Slater, and gorge calories at C.P.K."

Dionne said, "I'm in."

Tai got even more emotional. "You guys," she said, hugging us.

We had done the top tier of the Beverly Center and were sitting down for a bite. Our waiter introduced himself as Miles. He wore a black T-shirt wriggling with pecs and lats. It was hard to retain the specials he recited, but we were almost ready.

"How about angel hair?" I said.

"With sauce on the side?" De asked.

"Yeah."

"Okay, Miles," I said, "we want angel hair pasta, no oil, no butter, no cheese, with sauce on the side and a green salad, no dressing, with balsamic vinegar on the side and diet Coke with lime but no ice."

He got it all and left. "Survey says?" I asked De and Tai.

Tai studied Miles. "Doable. But I prefer longer hair, you know, like parted in the middle. Kind of dirty blondish . . ."

"Kind of Travis Birkenstockish?" I laughed.

"Why do you guys think he's such a bonehead? I mean, I can really talk to him. He's a ferocious good listener. And he goes for Marvin the Martian and all. We've got lots in common."

"Tai," De explained, "Travis has made an art of avoiding life. How can a man like that love?" Then she turned back to Miles. "Too puny. I like 'em big. I like a strong pair of arms, you know, all protective."

"I hate muscles," I said. "I like them to be protective cause they're smart, like my dad."

We moved from Miles to the other waiters and were just getting started on a table-by-table survey of the customers, when Tai went rigidly silent.

"What's wrong?" I asked.

"They're playing our song." She pointed to the speakers on the ceiling. "The one Elton and I danced to. You know, 'Slide, Slide, Slippity Slide.'" But she was too choked up to go on and burst into tears again.

I could tell that Tai's grieving period would be considerable unless I found someone to take Elton's place. The very next day I started shopping the school again. It looked depressingly like a bargain store rack. A row of identical boys in different sizes, all in big, fat sneakers, baggy pants, baggy shirts, and backward caps.

I don't mean to sound like a raging feminist, but when I think of all the time we spend on exercising, doing our hair, shopping, and make-up . . . whereas guys fall out of bed, put on a backward cap and expect us to swoon. I guess I'm a traitor to my generation, but the way guys look now does nothing for me.

Chapter 11

Not all my matchmaking efforts ended
in tragic failure. Mr. Hall and Miss Geist were
now a solid item. I saw them talking before the
start of Hall's class. I was at my desk, snipping a
hangnail, when they exchanged a good-bye buzz.

A few minutes into the hour, there was a knock
at the door. I looked up. My jaw hit the desk.
There in the doorway was James Dean. I mean, a
totally gorgeous rebel in a vintage fifties cocoa
gabardine shirt, stovepipe jeans rolled at the
cuffs, with a Sinatra-type hat pushed back on his
head. He was blue-eyed. He was slender. He was
grinning. He had nothing in common with the
off-the-rack set.

"This must be the elusive Christian Stovitz,"
Mr. Hall said.

"Where should I park?"

Hall pointed to the empty seat behind mine. "There's one, third back."

He sauntered over to it. After a beat, I took out my makeup mirror and positioned it so that I could see him. Watching his intelligent yet sleepy-eyed face, seeing him slick back the tousled sides of his hair helped me decide. I fully intended to find a guy for Tai. But I guessed there was no harm in getting one for myself also.

I knocked a pencil off my desk. Christian reached down to get it. His eyes traveled from my legs to my face. He smiled up at me. "Nice stems."

I felt my face flush. "Thanks," I managed to say.

He fastened me with a Rhett Butler grin.

"Cher," Mr. Hall said.

"Present," I answered.

"Yes, we established that during attendance. It's time for your oral. Your original oral on Violence in the Media."

"Excuse me," I said to Christian. I got up and went to the head of the class. "So, okay. The attorney general says there's too much violence on TV and that should stop. She says people will watch violent TV and want to try it. But even if you took off all the violent shows, people could still see violence on the news. So until mankind is peaceful enough to not have violence on the news, there's no point taking it out of shows that need it for entertainment value. Thank you."

I pulled a pretty good share of whistles and

applause. Then Mr. Hall asked for comments. Elton raised his hand. "Mr. Hall, my foot hurts. Can I go to the nurse?"

Hall nodded. Elton fake limped out of class.

"Christian, any thoughts?" Mr. Hall asked.

Christian shifted in his seat. He leaned back lazily, penny loafers in the aisle, and said, "Solid angle on the topic. Strictly locked-up legit."

Favorable! Though Mr. Hall looked confused. He called on Travis next.

"Two very enthusiastic thumbs up," Travis said. "Fine holiday fun."

"Hello," said Amber. "Was I the only one listening? I mean, I thought it reeked."

"I think," I said, "that's your designer imposter perfume."

The bell rang. Everyone raced out. Christian patted me as he left. "I dug it," he said.

De and I maneuvered for space in front of the Ladies Room mirror. We were touching up our hair between classes. "Do you remember Christian Stovitz?" I asked.

"No. Describe."

"Major studmuffin. I mean if I *were* the type who likes high school guys . . ."

"Christian? Slim. Blue-eyed. Jimmy Dean type. Vintage clothing. Weird hat?"

Amber's entrance brought conversation to a screeching halt.

"Cher, can I borrow your mascara?" she asked.

I lent it to her. She examined it with disappointment. "Maybelline?"

"Shuffle the cards and *deal,*" De told her.

"By the way, Amber," I said, "thanks for trashing my report."

"I'm sorry, I'm very honest. I *have* to say what I think."

De gave that some thoughtful attention. "Why?" she asked.

Amber ignored her and continued fluffing her frizzies.

"I didn't get this month's *Teen* yet," I said. "Is big hair back?"

"You are so junior high." Amber sniffed. Then, sensing that popular opinion was running against her, she flipped me my mascara and flounced out.

"Do you think it would be in bad taste for me to investigate a potential hottie of my own," I asked De when we were alone again. "I mean, before I get back to work on Tai's case?"

Her eyebrows shot up. "Christian? Go, girl!"

"I mean, I won't go overboard or anything. I'll just do what any normal girl would," I told her. "I'll send myself flowers, candy, and love notes so he can see how desired I am, in case he doesn't know."

"And if he makes any attempt at humor, you have to pretend he's hysterical."

"He sits behind me, can I borrow that strappy backless dress of yours?"

For the rest of the week, I followed the game

plan. I'd enter Mr. Hall's room shortly after Christian did. And each day, I'd acknowledge the rose or the chocolates or the lacy Hallmark on my desk with a mysterious yet modest smile.

I shared the chocolates with the whole class. "Thanks, Princess," Christian said, plucking a truffle from the box.

"Got one to spare?" he asked about the roses. "You probably get enough to open your own florist shop."

I laughed and chose one for him. "Smells almost as good as you do," he said, before he broke off the stem and tucked the flower into the lapel of his jacket.

On Friday, as we were leaving class, he caught up with me. "Hey, Duchess."

"Yeah?"

He offered me some gum. "So are you rationed this weekend?"

"Huh?" I asked, accepting a piece of calorie-loaded Juicy Fruit. Hello, whatever happened to NutraSweet?

"Like Saturday," Christian said. "I'm new, but maybe you've got an in with the heavy clambakes."

"Well, my ex-stepbrother's frat is having a party," I remembered. "The Breeders are playing."

"Solid," he said.

Saturday night, our house was crawling with young lawyers. Daddy had a case that had to be solved right away, so his legal assistant, Logan, some clerks, and Josh came to help him go through a gazillion depositions. When the doorbell rang, they all ignored it.

"Daddy!" I yelled from upstairs. "I can't just open it. I have to make him wait awhile."

Daddy yelled back, "Then he can wait outside."

"Josh! Pleeeeeeease!"

Reluctantly, Josh dragged himself across the entrance hall. I watched from behind the powder room door at the top of the stairs. Christian looked amazingly fifties. He was wearing a two-tone jacket and his Frank Sinatra hat. "What do you hear?" he said, sauntering past Josh.

Josh took Christian's hat off and handed it to him. "She's not ready," he said without enthusiasm, and walked away.

Christian went over to Daddy. "Hey, man. Nice pile of bricks you got here."

Daddy ignored Christian's extended hand. "You drink?" he asked.

"No thanks, I'm cool," Christian said.

"I'm not offering, idiot!" Daddy growled. "I'm asking *if* you drink. What do you think, I give alcohol to teenage drivers taking my daughter out?"

"No, man. The paternal vibe. I can dig it."

"What's your story, kid?" Daddy looked Christian over suspiciously. "You think the death of Sammy Davis left an opening in the Rat Pack?"

It wasn't going all that well. I decided I'd better make my entrance immediately. I glided down the stairs in my short but shimmering slip dress. Josh was staring at me as I kissed Christian hello. I caught him giving Daddy a look.

"You're not letting her go like that, are you?" he whispered.

"Cher, get in here," Daddy said, turning on his heel and heading into his office.

I shot Josh a squinchie with my eyes. "Zup, Daddy?" I asked.

"What is that thing you're wearing?"

"A dress."

"Says who?"

"Calvin Klein," I said.

"It looks like underwear. Go put something over it."

"Duh, I was just going to," I said. On the way out, I said to Josh, who was in his lumberjack togs again, "You organized this benefit, aren't you going?"

"No, I hate dancing." I gave him a look. "Okay, I'm lousy at it," he admitted. "It makes me look like a marionette."

"I'm shocked." I brushed past him. I was halfway up the stairs when I heard Daddy say to Christian, "No drinking and driving. If anything happens to Cher, I've got a forty-five and a shovel. I doubt anyone would miss you."

He's so protective. When I was a kid, Daddy had an intercom system put in my room so he could hear me from his office. The old speaker was tucked away now deep inside my walk-in closet. I was in there looking for a sheer cover-up to throw over the slip dress when I spotted the intercom. For old time's sake, I threw the switch. Josh's voice came through.

"I don't like him," I thought I heard him say.

"What's to like?" Daddy sounded preoccupied. "Where's the Chiate file?"

"Don't you think it's weird to see Cher going out?" Josh persisted.

"Why? She's always been very sociable."

"I mean, just a few years ago she was playing with Barbies."

"And you were playing with trucks," Daddy pointed out.

"When guys see her in that dress, they'll think she's a woman."

"Settle down, Grandpa," Daddy said.

"And that little Frank Sinatra Junior . . . Maybe I should go to the party."

"If you feel—"

Josh cut him off. "Nah, it's okay. I'll stay."

I was on my way out of the room when the speaker squawked again. It was Josh. "Maybe I ought to go keep an eye on her," he said. Then, "Nah, you need me here, right?"

I flipped off the switch and hurried downstairs.

"Man, your father's scary," Christian said on the way to the car.

"Isn't he?" I said proudly.

We got in. "You like Billie Holiday?" he asked.

"I love him."

He put on a tape, and we headed for Westwood.

Chapter 12

I could see why Josh chose this fraternity, I thought, as Christian and I made our entrance. The frat house was packed. The music was loud. There was a disco ball suspended from the ceiling, sending out fractured sparks of light. No one was dancing.

"Groovy," Christian said, after checking out the rotating ball. He slipped his shades on, and we went through the house to the pool area. There was a single tree out back. It was pretty puny. Marky Mark must have planted it. And someone had decided to disguise the fact that it was fatally ill by dressing it up in colored lights. There were kegs of beer set up under it. A band, plugged into enormous scratchy speakers, started to play.

"Come on, let's dance," Christian said.

"But no one else is."

"So we'll be the first."

"I've got to wait for Tai," I said quickly. "I mean, she won't know anyone." I looked around. "Tai should like someone here. There's so many cute guys."

Christian lowered his shades and looked around the pool. "I'll say," he said cheerfully.

A yelping sound cut through the music. I turned to see Tai flying backward, as if she'd made her entrance on a skateboard that had skidded out from under her. There was no skateboard in sight. Only Tai's shoulder-bag strap, which had gotten caught on a doorknob and sent her sailing.

"There she is," I told Christian.

Tai scrambled up and came over. "I'm dying of embarrassment."

"No one saw," I said.

"Now all night I'll be known as 'that girl who fell on her butt.'"

"Tai, no one noticed."

A college guy walked by. "Are you okay, miss?" he asked.

Tai looked down and mumbled, "Yeah, thanks." She raised her head after he left, and gasped.

I followed her eyes. Elton had just walked through the door—accompanied by Amber. I was stunned. What was going on here? Had someone posted a party invite on the Beverly

Hills High bulletin board? There was little consolation in the fact that Amber was wearing a hideous, furry white jacket.

"What's up?" Christian asked, checking them out. "Hey, isn't that Elton with Return to the Planet of the Apes?"

"I don't believe it," Tai said. "He's going with Amber."

"Oh, he probably just gave her a ride," I said, a second before Elton and Amber started kissing. "Well, it just proves what I've always said, 'The easier you fall in and out of love, the more shallow a person you are.'"

"Do you think she's pretty?" Tai asked.

"Tscha!" I said, making a face. "She's a full-on Monet."

"A what?"

"Like the paintings. Okay from far away, but up close just a big mess. Let's ask a guy. Christian, what do you think of Amber?"

He took his time. "Hagsville," he decided.

"See?" I told Tai.

"Dig this, they're charging for brews. Can you mash me a fin? I'll pay you back," Christian said. I dug a five out of my bag and gave it to him, and he went over to the kegs.

"Christian is so cute," Tai said.

We watched him. Girls passed and eyed him, but he ignored them. Then he got into an *extremely* pleasant conversation with the guy selling beer. Who, I noticed, was absolutely adorable.

"He's really falling in love with you. I mean, look how he ignores every other girl. Hey," Tai said, "should I wear my plaid shirt over my T-shirt?"

"No, tie it around your waist."

Christian returned and pulled me out to the dance floor. In no time, practically everyone in the place had turned to watch him dance. He was outstanding, a killer dancer. Over his shoulder, I caught a glimpse of someone who looked just like Josh. The guy was talking to an older man, the only one at the party.

It *was* Josh. I hadn't even noticed him arrive, but there he was, and he had managed to find the only grown-up in the house to talk to. Like he was deliberately trying to not have fun. He spotted me, and we waved to each other. And then I noticed Tai. She was the only girl on the outskirts of the floor. A few guys were looking her over, but all of them decided against dancing with her.

The band was kicking. Christian was the hottest guy there. I knew my outfit was drop-dead cool But my enjoyment was put on pause because I could see that Tai was miserable. With each passing guy, she looked more defeated. She tried her shirt over her shoulder, tied around her waist, tucked in like a bustle. Nothing worked. All of a sudden, Josh grabbed her hand and took her to the dance floor. His dancing was beyond awful, it was painful.

"Look at Josh," I said to Christian. "He said he *never* dances."

"I can see why."

"No, he's doing a props so Tai wouldn't be left out. He's totally gallant."

"Oh," Christian said. "I dig."

Tai and Josh left the floor a couple of minutes later. Christian and I danced for hours. Then he excused himself. The crowd was beginning to thin out. Josh came over to Tai and me. "How you guys holding up?" he asked.

"I'm *so* ready to leave," I admitted.

"I'm tired," Tai said.

"Okay, I'll get Christian and we'll go," I told them. I found him talking with the bartender. The guy was muscle beach brawny, so I was kind of shocked to hear him giving like a museum-headphone lecture about local art and artists. Christian was deep into it.

"You ready to go?" I asked.

"Now?"

I didn't want to mention my curfew, so I said, "Well, my trainer's coming real early."

"Aww," he sort of groaned, disappointed.

Josh's hearing was a lot better than his dancing. He was over in a second. "I can take the girls home," he volunteered.

"No, that's okay," said Christian, but I could tell he really wanted to stay.

"It's all right, Christian," I said. "Really, you stay."

"You sure?" He was so cute. He tilted his head and stared at me like my being sure was the most important thing in the world to him.

"Of course."

"Thanks, man," he told Josh, "you've got my marker." Then he gave me a kiss on the cheek. "You're a real-down girl. I'll ring you tomorrow," he said.

After we dropped Tai off, I thanked Josh for dancing with her. "Have you seen any positive changes in her?" I asked.

"Oh, certainly. Under your tutelage she's exploring the challenging world of bare midriffs."

What did I expect? I rifled through his incredibly boring tape collection.

"So you didn't want to make a night of it with the Ring-a-Ding kid?" he said.

"Yeah, right. Daddy wouldn't go too ballistic. And it's not like he's going to sleep or anything."

"Not if they're going to finish those depos," Josh said.

"You know what would be *sooo* dope? If we got them some really delicious take-out. I'll bet they haven't eaten."

Josh gave me this look like, my-oh-my. "That would be quite decent of us," he agreed. "Let's do it."

We marched into the house with sacks of food. The legal elves saw us coming and practically tore the bags out of our hands. The midnight snack totally revived the lawyers, and Daddy was way grateful. Of course, I had to grab the bypass burger out of his hands, but I gave him a very decent salad instead.

I know it sounds mental, but sometimes I have more fun at home vegging out than when I go partying. Maybe it's 'cause my party clothes are so binding. What*ever*. That night, I got into my baggy sweats, and Josh and I hung out in the den, watching *Ren and Stimpy*. I was doing up my hair with wavy rods.

"Hey, don't get your hair in the cheese puffs," he warned me, grabbing the bag. "I'm just curious, Cher. How many hours of the day do you spend grooming yourself?"

"Some people aren't lucky enough to be as naturally adorable as you are," I said.

"You're making me blush."

"See," I told him. "Now, I'd need makeup for that." I tried to get the Chee•tos bag back. Josh was hogging it. The phone rang and I picked it up.

"Hello . . . Oh, hi, Gail," I said. It was Josh's mom calling long-distance.

He started furiously pantomiming that he didn't want to talk to her. I extended an open palm. He surrendered the Chee•tos. "No, he's not here," I told her. "Did you try the dorm? Uh-huh, okay, 'bye."

"What's up?" I asked him after I hung up the phone.

"She's going to tell me to come home for spring break."

"So? What's wrong with that? No one will be at school."

"Yeah, but husband number four is in the house, and his idea of acting like a family is to criticize me."

"Whereas my father's idea of acting like a family is to yell at everyone."

"Ah, that's just how Mel talks," he said. Josh's real dad took off for South America in the early eighties with suitcases of savings and loan cash. Funny, I'd never really thought about it, but Josh hadn't seen his father for almost as long as I hadn't seen my mom.

"So what are you going to do? Hang around an empty campus for two weeks?" I asked him.

"I don't mind."

"That's stupid. Come here. Use your old room. I'll heat the pool, and there's going to be a bunch of parties."

"Nah," Josh said.

"Why not?"

"You've got your whole social whirl going. I don't want to get in the way."

"You won't get in the way," I assured him.

"How much fun can you have with a brother type tagging along?"

"Josh! You're not my brother."

"You know what I mean."

"Come on, you need a little enjoyment. It'll replenish you for finals, okay?"

He grabbed back the Chee•tos. "Okay." Then he shook his head and laughed. "I can't believe

I'm taking advice from someone who watches cartoons."

"It's *Ren and Stimpy,*" I pointed out. "They're way existential."

He gave me this shocked look. "Do you know what you're talking about?"

"No. Why, do I sound like I do?"

We both laughed then, and watched TV.

Chapter 13

Christian had said he'd call me on Sunday, which in boy time meant around Thursday. So you can imagine my astonishment when I actually heard from him the next day. I was in my father's room, choosing outfits for him and laying them out on his bed. My portable phone rang. It was parked on the night table. It's black and sits straight up like the slab that made the apes get smart in *2001*.

"What's the plan, Stan?" Christian asked the minute I said hello.

"Well, Daddy's got to go away for a few days, so I'm getting him packed up."

"Coolsville. Let's throw a bender."

"Thank you, but I stand to inherit this house,

and my decorating ideas do not include teenage destruction," I informed him.

"So you're going to be by yourself in that big, lonely house."

"Yeah . . ."

"You need someone to protect you? Keep you company?"

"Sure . . ."

"Then, I'll come by with some videos," he said, and hung up.

Beyond belief, I thought, a date alone with Christian, and Daddy will be gone. I sent for reinforcements.

Dionne showed up as Daddy's cab pulled out of the driveway. Together we did a light check of the den. We moved lamps around and flicked them on and off. We changed bulbs from white to pale pink to party yellow to waterfront red until we came up with the perfect formula. One that was complimentary cosmetically, but where you didn't need a cane to get around.

Next we worked on costume decisions. My room was littered with clothing and photographs. I'd try on a new outfit, and Dionne would take front and side Polaroids of me in it. We shuffled through the pictures for hours, narrowing the choices to three dynamite possibilities.

Also I decided there had to be the smell of something baking. It's like a very basic thing with men. It reminds their subconscious how much they need females. So Lucy mixed up some cookie dough, and De and I tossed globs of it onto baking trays, which I was supposed to pop into the oven about fifteen minutes before Christian showed up.

I was so excited that my face got all flushed. De was trying to do my makeup. "I'm still all red," I complained.

"I'm trying to make you as white as I can," she said, dabbing on more foundation. "Calm down, girlfriend. You're totally melting."

Even I was impressed with the job De did. We slapped a viciously limp high five, and then she had to go. Murray was going to give her driving lessons. I walked her downstairs. "You know," I said, "I'm so glad I never went out with a high school boy before. I mean, Christian is brutally hot, and I'll remember tonight forever."

De gave me a hug, and took off. I tossed the cookie tray into the oven, then ran upstairs to finish my hair.

I looked gorgeous. I answered the door, confident that Christian would be knocked out. He was. He whistled at me. I sort of expected a kiss, but he walked past me and sniffed the air and said, "Is something burning?"

"Oh, no!" I shrieked. I ran into the kitchen. The cookies were past tense. Black smoke was billowing from the oven. Christian had followed me in. "Ah, honey," he said, "you baked."

I was trying to wave the smoke away with a couple of dish towels. He took them out of my hands and led me out of the kitchen. "Come on," he said gently, "show me the rest of your pad."

I showed him around downstairs, and then we went out back to the pool area. It's riddled with sculpture. Christian wandered from statue to statue, way impressed. "Henry Moore . . . Calder . . ." he recited.

"They're ferociously famous."

"Oh, wow, a Lichtenstein! This is an *important* piece."

I wasn't certain what that meant, but I wanted to appear interested. "And pretty, too," I ventured.

"Fabulous patina," he commented on another one.

Art is not an area I'm burningly confident about. "Fabulous," I said, hoping to move things along. "Want to go swimming?"

He glanced at the pool. At me. Then back up at the house. "Ooh, let's watch the movies," he decided.

"Den or upstairs?" I offered.

"Biggest screen?"

"Master bedroom, come on."

He popped a tape into the VCR, and we flopped down on a mile of bed. Christian had a thing for Tony Curtis, so we had to watch *Spartacus*. And he wanted to see it all the way through. It's a really long movie, a serious epic. It was at this scene where Laurence Olivier, who's wretchedly rich, is like examining Tony Curtis, who's his slave. Tony is wearing just a loincloth and lace-up sandals.

"You just don't see faces like that anymore," Christian said. He was all the way over on the other side of the bed. I scooted over to him.

"Like in old Rome?" I asked.

"No, like in old Hollywood," he said.

I kind of stretched and put my feet next to his. He pulled away. "Oh, sorry," I said quickly, "my feet were cold."

He grabbed a plaid cashmere blanket and covered my legs, tucking them in so tight I couldn't move them at all. "Better?"

I was deeply disappointed, but I managed a smile. "Thanks."

"Ooh, watch this part, watch!" Christian moved my face toward the TV. Even though he had me lashed like a mummy, I wriggled into the most alluring pose I could. Unfortunately, I had no idea how near the edge I was. Instead of turning him on, I tumbled off the bed.

"You okay?" he said as I lay struggling on the floor, fighting my way out of the cashmere cocoon.

"Fine." It was getting harder to smile. I tore off the blanket and threw it on the leather lounger. Then, smoothing my clothes, I said, "As long as I'm up, can I get you a drink? Some wine?"

"No thanks," Christian said, not taking his

eyes off Laurence and Tony. As an afterthought, he added, "You ever notice how wine makes people feel like they have to be sexy or something?"

I felt a furious blush creep up under De's makeup. "That's okay," I said forlornly. I hadn't meant to sound dejected.

Suddenly Christian looked at me. "Cher? I didn't mean . . . Cher, I know you weren't trying to . . . Listen, I'm getting tired." He did this totally bogus stretch and yawn thing, then sprang off the bed. "This movie's a lot longer than I remembered." He pressed the eject button and grabbed the tape. "Cher, you look really great. Did I tell you how I love that outfit? You have the best taste. The best pad here. High style."

"I could make some coffee if you like," I said lamely.

He was backing out of the bedroom. "Oh, no thanks . . . I've got . . . an ulcer!" He clutched his stomach.

I was confused. "Then how come you had all those cappuccinos before?"

"Oh . . . well . . ." We were in the upstairs hall. Christian was at the head of the stairs. "Foam," he fairly shouted. "You know, ulcers. Foam. Cappuccino foam. Best thing for them."

Duh, finally I got it. He was not tired. He was not sick. He just wanted to leave. No amount of makeup could keep that realization from showing on my face. All of a sudden I felt like one of those plastic dolls where you get to see all the body parts inside. I felt like Christian was seeing my heart and my hurt. And it felt awful.

We were at the front door. I could tell he felt bad, too. I tried smiling again. It sort of worked.

"You're great," he said. "Are we friends?"

"Yeah . . ."

He pointed to his cheek. "Then knock me a kiss."

I kissed his cheek. He grabbed his hat, did a little trick with it, and left.

Chapter 14

Hop in, dude," Dionne said.

She and Murray stopped by the next day to pick me up. De was at the wheel of the BMW. Murray was raving. It was the usual driving lesson drill.

I slid into the backseat. "I don't get it. What did I do wrong? What's the matter with me?" I asked, continuing the phone conversation De and I had begun at 10 A.M. "Plus why did he want me to kiss him good-bye? I mean, it wasn't your fault. The makeup was flawless. Maybe I'm not smart enough for him. I don't mean like debate smart, I mean, you know art smart, movie smart. I didn't even know *Spartacus* was a classic. He's very into that stuff."

"Woman, keep your eye on the road," Murray

119

warned De as a forest green Jag started beeping frantically at us. "That mirror is for checking your rear, not conversing!"

Dionne made a sharp turn to the right to avoid the Jaguar and wound up humping over a curb. It was just a little bump. Murray put his hand on his head, dragged his cap down, and held it over his face for a minute. "That was a lawsuit. That was a near-miss, multimillion-dollar, head-on, mortgage-your-mama's-big-house lawsuit," he grumbled furiously.

"Maybe he really was tired," De said.

"Maybe my hair got really flat during the course of the evening."

"Maybe he wants to get to know you better."

"You checking your mirror?" Murray said.

"Yeah, yeah," said Dionne.

"Just keep checking your mirror."

"I suppose it wasn't meant to be," I said. "I mean, he dresses and dances better than I do. What would I bring to the relationship?"

"Look down the road. Take in the whole picture." For a minute I thought Murray was talking to me, but it was Dionne he meant.

"Maybe I was too available. Guys like to do the conquering."

"Get into the left lane," Murray told De.

She swerved toward the next lane, barely escaping a collision.

"WHAT ARE YOU DOING?!" Murray screamed.

"You said, get into the lane."

"That means you follow the procedure for changing lanes. Do you remember the procedure?"

"Yes, I remember the *procedure.*"

"Then switch back to the right lane. What's the first thing you do?"

"I put on the signal," she said impatiently. She flipped up the little stick on the steering wheel column. The wipers went on. Murray did this totally exaggerated groan. De looked down to find the signal switch, and the car weaved.

"WATCH THE ROAD," he commanded.

De's head snapped back up, eyes glued to the window again. Murray found the signal.

"Now I look in the mirror . . ." De demonstrated. "And then I glance at the blind spot." She turned both her head and the car.

"You glance with your head, not the whole car. Woman, you can *not* drive."

"I'm not trying to hear that," De said.

"You better be trying."

"Actually," I said, "falling in love is a big decision. I can't believe I was so capricious about it. I was thinking of giving myself to him, utterly."

Murray turned around. "To who?" he demanded protectively.

"Christian."

"What are you talking about?" Murray said, "You don't have what it takes to give it utterly to Christian."

"Excuse me?"

"Are you blind? Christian is a cake-boy."

"A what?"

"A disco-dancing, latte-sipping, Streisand ticket-holding, Oscar Wilde–reading, friend of Dorothy. You get it?"

De and I sputter-laughed, then exchanged looks in the rearview mirror. Our mouths flopped open. You could read Can It Be True?! on our faces.

"Not even!" I said. "How can that be?"

"He does know how to dress himself," Dionne said after reexamining the situation.

"I'm buggin'," I said, curling up in a corner of the backseat, hugging myself, trying to think things through. Finally I said, "I feel like such a bonehead."

Murray turned back around. "YOU'RE GETTING ON THE FREEWAY!" he screamed, "QUICK! GET OUT OF THIS LANE!"

He was right. De was in the lane heading for the on-ramp. Now she was frantically looking for the turn signal.

"NOW! NOW! NOW! Forget the procedure!"

Dionne was checking the mirror, glancing to her right, trying to signal. "I can't," she wailed at last. "It's too fast." I sat up and put on my seat belt. De freaked. "OH, NO, THE FREEWAY!"

We hit the freeway screaming, all three of us. Then Murray took control. "When I tell you, go to the right."

Dionne was crying. I was still screaming. "Get

your head down," Murray ordered me. I ducked. "Okay . . . Now. Go."

De jerked into the other lane.

"Good girl," Murray said. "It's okay. We'll be off soon." There was an exit up ahead, and we were in the right lane for it now. "Here we go, that's it," Murray guided De.

She drove off the freeway and pulled over and stopped. She was shaking. Murray opened his arms to her. She threw herself into them. All of a sudden, they were hugging and crying and kissing desperately. They were affirming their love with a passion that comes only from a near-death experience.

And I was buckled up in the backseat, alone.

The revelation about Christian being ineligible as a long-term huggie didn't bum me totally. I knew he'd meant what he said. He did think I was great. He admired my clothes, my taste, my style, my house, and Daddy's art collection. I could see that Christian would become a thorough fun friend. But watching De and Murray's frantic front-seat reconciliation, I realized how much I wanted a boyfriend of my own.

Chapter 15

Where's Tai?" Christian asked.

It was a couple of weeks after the freeway follies. We were on the escalator heading for the top tier of the mall. "She met some random guys at the Footlocker," I told him, "and escorted them to the food court."

We spotted her over at a corner table surrounded by homey wannabes. They were generic Duh guys, sporting baggy pants and attitude. There was enough smoke mushrooming over their table to call a smog alert.

"Where does she find these Barneys?" I asked.

Christian grabbed my hand and headed right to the cappuccino stand. "Yumsville, it's java world," he said. We picked up a couple of coffees

124

and sat down. "Okay, think back," he said, digging through the shopping bags we'd accumulated. "That jacket at Traffic—was it James Dean or Jason Priestley?"

"Christian, you *have* to get it," I assured him.

"Really?"

"Carpe diem! You looked hot!"

We heard Tai screaming and looked over at her table. She was standing up now, laughing ferociously as she flirted with the rowdies. "Could they be more generic?" I said.

Suddenly one of the guys picked Tai up and ran over to the railing with her. Tai was clutching him, working hard on keeping up the shrieking, good-natured laughter, until he hauled her over the railing, threatening her with a two-story drop. "Adam! Put me down! *Stop!*" she started screaming.

Christian jumped up and tore over to them. He grabbed the guy from behind and spun him around. Adam dropped Tai safely on the ground. She scrambled over to me, and we stood there hugging, while Christian went after him.

"You brain-dead moron!" Christian yelled, trashing Adam with a single shot to the stomach. "You could've killed her!"

The other boys started tearing Christian off Adam. "Chill out." "Hey, it was just a joke," they were yelling. "Cool it."

Someone spotted a security guard, and the boys took off. Tai fell into Christian's arms. "Are you okay?" he asked her.

"Yeah, I'm fine," she snuffled into his shoulder.

"Your heart is pounding."

"Yeah, I know."

"Let's get you home for some R and R," Christian said gently.

"R and R? What are those?" Tai asked.

They headed for the escalator together. People were clucking and cooing all around them. I trailed behind, trying to balance my purse and packages, Tai's jacket, and Christian's twenty shopping bags. Considering how clueless she was, Tai certainly had the damsel-in-distress thing down.

Soon everyone was talking about Tai's Brush with Death. Mornings, she was mobbed in the Quad. Noontime, kids fought to sit at her table. She'd become the full-out flavor of the month.

"Hey, is it true some gang members tried to shoot Tai in the mall?" Summer asked me.

I was crossing the Quad on my way to meet Tai for lunch. "No," I said.

"That's what everyone is saying," Summer insisted.

I waved a *W* at her. "What*ever,*" I said.

My regular table was totally filled with awe-struck kids interviewing Tai. I heard snatches of annoying conversation as I approached. "Was there like a montage of all the scenes of your life?" someone was asking her.

"Not exactly a montage," Tai responded

thoughtfully, clearly aware of the tremendous responsibility a star has to her public. "But it's funny how something like that makes you stop and think about what's really important." She flicked her hair, then noticed me standing there.

"Hey, guys, move down for Cher," she commanded.

A few kids shifted, leaving me a generous three inches of bench. Dionne and Murray were across the table. Ever since the freeway episode, they'd been clinging to one another like a couple of Velcro strips. They didn't even see me sit down.

"Where was I?" Tai returned her attention to her rapt fans.

"You were thinking about what was really important," someone reminded her, someone in leather pants and a stringy-haired white bolero jacket. It was Amber! Oh, no, even Amber was sucking up to Tai.

"Yeah, your mind just sort of gets real clear when you think you're going to die," Tai continued.

"I know." I tried to join the conversation. "When I was held up, *at gunpoint—*"

"Excuse me," the kid next to me said, cutting me off. He got up, and a girl quickly sat down and leaned across me to catch every golden word of Tai's.

"Hey, Tai," I called.

She turned to me.

"I was planning on going to Tower and getting something for Christian," I said.

"Uh-huh."

"Like some CDs of that music he listens to. Sort of a present, like. Want to do that with me?" I must have sounded brutally desperate. I could see it in Tai's eyes, which were suddenly full of embarrassing sympathy.

"Oooh, yeah," she said. "Sure, I mean. I owe him my life."

Everyone started nodding and clucking and echoing snips of Tai's words. "Yeah, yeah, right" and "She owes him her life."

"So I'll get you after school—"

"Oh, not today," Tai clarified. "I'm going to Melrose with Amber."

She might as well have said, she was going to Oz with the Monkey Queen. I couldn't believe it. I swallowed what was left of my pride and asked, "How about tomorrow?"

"You think we could do it . . . next Monday? My week's filling up pretty fast."

I was pretty bruised, but I managed to keep a smile in place. Then Murray split, and De, my best friend Dionne, totally ignored me and turned with shining eyes to share her love secrets with Tai.

They were giggling ferociously together when Travis suddenly showed up.

"Oh, swoon, here's your boyfriend," De kidded Tai.

"Hey, Tai, you like seafood?" Travis asked.

"Yes . . ."

"Okay. 'See' food." He opened his mouth and showed her what was left of his lunch.

"Ugh!" Tai said.

"Could you shove down?" Travis asked one of the kids, trying to make room for himself next to Tai.

"Hello," Tai said coldly. "Don't you slackers prefer the stairwell?"

I was shocked. Tai sounded so cold . . . so judgmental . . . so . . . like me! I watched Travis schlepp away glumly. I actually felt bad for him.

Dionne and Tai resumed their giggling and whispers. "Murray hasn't yelled at me since the freeway," I heard De confide. "Do you think that's a danger sign or what?"

What was happening? Dionne asking Tai for advice, Tai being the most popular girl in school. It was like some sort of alternate universe. And, on top of everything else, I was totally wigged out because it was time to take my driving test, and I knew I had just two days left to put together my most responsible-looking ensemble.

Chapter 16

Saturday morning my room was in brutal disarray. I still hadn't found the proper outfit. Between Tai's soaring popularity, De's casual desertion, and the fact that I had about an hour left before the test, I was totally stressed.

"LUCY! LUUUUCY!" I screamed.

Josh and some of the other law drones were working on depos in my father's office.

"Lucy! Where's my white collarless shirt from Fred Segal?"

I could feel Josh's disapproving gaze following me from the office door. I turned on him, a squinchie already narrowing my eyes. To my surprise he looked . . . well, more disappointed than disapproving.

"She's in the kitchen," he said.

I hurried in. "It's probably at the cleaners," Lucy called from behind the counter. She was loading breakfast dishes into the dishwasher.

"But today's the driving test, and it's my most capable-looking."

Lucy slammed the dishwasher shut and straightened up. "Okay, I'll call them."

"It's too late now," I snapped. "And we got another notice from the fire department about clearing out the bush."

Josh sauntered into the kitchen in search of a snack. I ignored him and said to Lucy, "You were going to tell José to do it."

"He's your gardener," Lucy complained. "Why don't you tell him?"

"Yeah, right. You know I don't speak Mexican."

Lucy threw down her dish towel. "I am not Mexican," she said, and left.

"Oh, great. Now, can you tell me what that was about?" I whirled on Josh.

"Lucy is from El Salvador."

"So?"

"It's an entirely different country, Cher."

"What does that matter?"

"You get upset if someone thinks you live below Sunset."

"Yeah, yeah, I'm always wrong. Everything's my fault."

"You are such a brat," Josh said. Grabbing a spoon for his yogurt, he left. I started to follow him but changed my mind. Instead I went into the dining room where Lucy was staring out the window.

"Lucy, I'm sorry. The driving test is making me mental." I hugged her.

"I know," she said, hugging me back. "Don't worry. Good luck on your test."

An overwhelming sense of ickiness followed me, even as I waited in line at the Department of Motor Vehicles with my written test and a gazillion forms in my hand. I knew I was sorry about upsetting Lucy. But me and Luce never stay mad long. No, there was something else bothering me. It was hard to put my finger on it. It had something to do with that dream about my mother, the one where she shook her head and called me clueless. Like she was disappointed in me. Just like that look on Josh's face this morning.

Josh thinking I was mean or something was making me postal—which I knew would *not* improve my driving skills.

The guy who was testing me looked nervous before he even climbed into the Jeep. We were creeping along this shabby street, and I was all into why should I care what Josh thinks.

The tester said, "Move into the right lane."

I did, still wondering why I was letting what Josh said wig me out.

"Watch out for the BIKE RIDER!"

I swerved back into my lane, and this person on a bicycle whizzed by perfectly unharmed.

"Whoops, my bad," I told the tester. After that, I stayed in the middle of the road.

"What are you doing? You're taking up both lanes," he started in. "Police frown on that, you know. Get in the right lane."

Now he was getting me all nervous. "But I'm afraid I'll scrape the parked cars."

"You can't have the whole road to yourself."

So I started to go to my right, and, sure enough, I scraped a parked car. And, of course, then the tester starts yelling, "NOT SO CLOSE."

"Uh-oh, should I write them a note?" I asked.

"Pull over up here and turn off the engine."

"Okay. Cool. Start over, take two." I pulled over to the curb. "Want me to parallel park?"

He was filling out forms. "No. Let's just switch seats."

"Excuse me, are we going somewhere to make left-hand turns?"

"We're going back to the DMV."

"It's over?"

"It's over," he said.

"How'd I do?"

"How'd you do?" said the tester. "Hmmm, let's see." He checked his notes. "You can't park, switch lanes, make right-hand turns, make left-hand turns, you've damaged private property, and almost killed someone. Offhand, I'd say . . . you failed."

"Failed???" I couldn't believe it. "Can't we just start over? I'm kind of having a personal problem, so I had my mind somewhere else. And

you saw how that bike rider came out of nowhere, right? I swear, I'll concentrate. I drive
really good usually . . ."

"So what was this? A special occasion?"

"Isn't there anyone else I can talk to," I asked.
It was clear he was not in the mood to negotiate.
"Is there a supervisor or something? I mean, you
can't be the absolute and final word in driver's
licenses."

"Girlie," he said, "as far as you're concerned,
I'm the messiah of the DMV. Now get out of the
car."

I returned home in a state of shock. I couldn't
believe it. I had failed my driving test. I had
failed at something that I couldn't talk my way
out of. I was just hating life.

My misery was interrupted by yelps of laughter. Without thinking, I followed the sounds
outside, to the edge of the terrace. There below
me, at the foot of a rolling expanse of manicured
lawn, were the last two people I wanted to see
me in this state of like almost defeat. Josh and
Tai . . . both of them . . . bumping into each
other . . . shrieking with laughter . . . enjoying
life!

"Hi," I called.

Tai glanced up. "Ay, you're home," she said.

"How does it feel to have a license?" Josh was
beaming.

"I wouldn't know. I failed the test."

"Bummer," Tai said, heading my way.

Josh just stared at me, with this leftover grin on his face.

"And spare me your lectures on what a big responsibility driving is and how you can't talk your way through it, okay?" I said to him.

"I didn't say anything."

"I can tell what you're thinking," I said, and went back into the house.

Tai waved good-bye to Josh and ran in after me. She was carrying this carton. She followed me into the den and set the box down on the coffee table where we'd once looked at self-improvement books together. Of course, that was before Tai became the victim-queen of Beverly Hills High.

"I'm glad you're here," she said. "There's something I want to do, and I'd like it if you were with me."

Someone had started a fire in the fireplace. Reflected in the massive screen of our home-entertainment center, the flames gave the room a cozy glow. "What's all this?" I asked, pointing at the box.

"This is junk that reminds me of Elton." She opened the lid. "But now I want to burn it, 'cause I am *so* over him."

I remembered how hard I'd tried to hook Tai up with Elton. I remembered the pain of rejection she'd suffered. At that moment, I looked at her and saw the old Tai again—naive, vulnerable, without guile or fashion sense.

"What's in there?" I asked, happy that she wanted my help, even on this day of dismal failure.

"Okay, remember when we were at the Val party and the clog knocked me out and he got a towel of ice to cure me?"

"Yeah."

"Well, I didn't tell you . . ." She pulled a wrinkled kitchen towel out of the carton. "I took it for a souvenir."

"You're kidding."

"No." She tossed the rag into the fire.

"Then, once my pen ran out, and I borrowed one from him." She threw the pen into the flames and took a cassette out of the box. "And remember the song playing when we danced? 'Slide, Slide, Slippity Slide'? I got the tape and listened to it every night."

"Wait!" I hollered, grabbing the cassette before she tossed it in the fire. "I'll take that." I threw it on the couch. "I'm really happy for you, Tai, but what brought on this surge of empowerment?"

"It's like I like someone new who is so amazing that he makes Elton look like a total loser."

"That's great," I said, breaking into a big happy grin.

"Yeah. Look, you've got to help me get Josh."

"Get Josh what?"

"You know what I mean. I know it's impossible, but you keep saying 'seize the day,' you know, carpe diem, and you're so smart at this stuff. Anyway, I passed the driver's test, and then the mall thing did wonders for my reputation. I feel like I deserve a guy I love. It's all because of you. You've been such a good friend." Tai gave me a grateful hug.

The big, happy grin was frozen on my face, but I felt sick suddenly. If I was so smart, how come I didn't know why the thought of Tai and Josh together made my stomach fall like an elevator in a Bruce Willis movie? And how come I never knew that carpe diem meant "seize the day"?

"Have you gotten any clues about whether he likes you?" I asked with this fraudulent super-calm.

"Oh, yeah!"

"Like what?"

"Little things, ya know?" Tai said. "Like how he always finds a reason to touch or tickle me, you know. Then, that night at his frat, he noticed how depressed I was so he asked me to dance and was real flirty and all."

I was still grinning. Tai said, "Are you okay?"

"Yeah . . . well, actually, I was really bad to-day," I said, "I had two mochaccinos. Now I feel like ralphing." The last sentence was so true. I know this sounds vicious, but suddenly I totally wished I'd never met Tai.

"College guys like less makeup, and he told me to read *Beyond Good and Evil*," she was bab-bling. "But it's too confusing so I'll get the Cliff's Notes."

"But, Tai, you don't really think you'd be

happy with Josh. I mean he's like, this school nerd."

"And what? I'm sort of a mentally challenged airhead?"

"Not even!" I said quickly. "I didn't say that."

"When it comes to guys, you think I'm interested in recycling your leftovers, but I'm not good enough for Josh?"

"I just don't think you . . . mesh well," I said.

"You don't think we mesh well? I mean, it's like, why am I even listening to you? You've never had a guy of your own, and you can't drive!"

"That was way harsh, Tai."

"Okay, okay, I'm sorry," she said angrily. "We'll talk when we've mellowed. I'm Audi!"

Tai stormed out of the den. I marched restlessly around the room, thinking, what did I do? I created a monster. I could feel the chunks rise to my throat. I had to get out.

Chapter 17

I didn't even change my clothes. I left the house and just began walking. Everything I thought and did was wrong. I had failed the driver's test. I'd been wrong about Elton. I was wrong about Christian. Josh hated me. It all boiled down to one inevitable conclusion—I was totally clueless.

Was this the teen angst I'd heard so much about, I asked myself as I walked blindly past the old hotels and weird mansions of Wilshire Boulevard. This Tai-and-Josh concept was wigging me more than anything. What was my problem? Tai was like, my pal. I certainly didn't begrudge her a boyfriend.

Instinctively, I had wandered onto Rodeo Drive. Not even shopping interested me, except for this one outfit I saw that was similar but not identical to Dionne's hottest two-piece leopard thing. It was all alone in this stark window, and it sidetracked me for a minute. I thought I'd just pop into the store and see if they had it in my size. They did.

What did Tai want with Josh anyway, I asked myself. Shifting the dress-shop package to my other hand, I pressed the Cross button on the traffic light at Santa Monica Boulevard. Josh dressed funny. He listened to complaint rock. He wasn't even cute in the conventional way. I mean, yes he had this thick, glossy, healthy dark hair and those expensive teeth and a longish, slightly dented, very masculine nose. And it was interesting the way no matter how often he shaved, you could always see this hint of beard along his strong jaw.

In the golden, late afternoon light, I passed this statue called *The Thinker*. It made me think of Josh. Imagine him with Tai, I thought. Josh holding Tai's hand. Tai making little jokes about him. I mean, I liked Tai, but she wouldn't make him happy. He needed someone smarter. Someone who could see through his raging philosophical outbursts and love him anyway.

As day faded into night, I trudged past the fountain on Wilshire and Santa Monica. There was something familiar about the scene—the fountain, the dark star-studded sky, me walking around, trying to figure things out. Then I remembered this video Christian had brought over. It was called *Gigi*. It was about this rich French guy who could have any girl he wanted. He gets all confused. He walks past this fountain in Paris. Suddenly he realizes he's in love with Gigi, this girl he's known since she was a kid. She's been growing up right under his nose all the time. The minute he gets it, that she's the one, the fountain goes off like fireworks, spurting all these colors.

That was what it reminded me of. Me walking around a fountain just like the French guy, only in Beverly Hills. Me thinking about someone who'd grown up right under my nose. Someone who'd helped me get over my loneliness. Someone who always showed up when I was in trouble. Someone who had brains and even sexy eyebrows, like Daddy.

That was when it hit me. "I . . . don't . . . believe it," I yelled. "I love *Josh!*" I paced back and forth in a total frenzy. "I am majorly, totally, furiously, crazy in love with Josh."

It was the worst thing that had ever happened to me. All of a sudden, I didn't know how to act around him. We were sitting on the couch, watching the news one night. Josh was all Chee•tos and Diet Coke, sprawled in his old khakis and a Trip Shakespeare T-shirt. I was relaxed as a board.

Ordinarily, if I wanted someone to like me, I'd send myself presents and strut around in my sexiest outfits. But for some reason I couldn't do that with Josh.

"Hey, what's with you?" he asked.

"What do you mean?"

"You're so quiet. You haven't made me watch *The Real World.*"

"I care about the news," I said.

"Since when?"

"Since now." I stared with deep concentration at the TV.

"You look confused," Josh said a minute later.

"I thought they declared peace in the Middle East," I said.

Josh laughed at me. I got up and walked out.

Great, I thought. I was turning into a dork, and Josh was flirting with Tai. What a revolting development! I loved somebody, and he loved someone else! It hurt! It just hurt . . . and I *hate* pain. What do people do with pain, I wanted to know. How do they make it stop?

I roamed past my father's office. He was working inside. I stepped in, then quickly backed out again. I couldn't bother him. He had so much to do. I kept drifting past his door and finally I headed in. Where else could I turn? But I got nervous and ducked out again.

"Cher, get in here," he called.

I did. "What's up, Daddy?" I said casually. He was in his shirtsleeves, wearing the red paisley suspenders I'd seen in *GQ* and the trousers to the Armani suit I'd picked out for him.

"What are you doing, dancing outside my

office?" he asked, glancing up from the pile of papers on his desk.

"Nothing. I just wanted to see if I could help."

"All right, come here," he said. He handed me a folder. "You can do this. Every time they mention a phone conversation on September third, you take this highlighter and mark it, you got that?"

"Okay." I sat down and started reading and marking.

When I looked up, Daddy was smiling at me. "Isn't this fun?"

"Yeah." I was trying to figure out the best way to bring up my problem.

"Daddy, did you ever have a situation you couldn't argue your way out of?" I asked him.

"Of course not, honey." I guess my shoulders really sagged, because then he said, "Tell me what the problem is, and we'll figure out how to argue it."

"I like this boy," I said after a minute.

"Uh-oh."

"And he likes someone else."

"How could that be?" Daddy said.

"I don't know, but I feel wretched."

"Well, obviously this young man is a moron. You're the prettiest girl in Beverly Hills. Anyway, I'm not sure I'd like you to be with such a stupid fellow."

"Actually," I said with my head down, fiddling with a corner of the file folder, "he's a smart guy. And like a do-gooder type, so I worried that all my after-school commitments—massage, leg waxing, personal trainer—weren't doing any good, you know? Like I'm just a well-dressed loser."

Daddy's shadow loomed over me. "Honey," he said, sounding almost as heartbroken as I felt. I looked up at him. He opened his arms to me, and I stood up and fell into them. "How can you say such things?" he asked, stroking my hair. "Who makes sure everybody in the house is happy? Who sees that I eat healthy? Who takes care of everyone around here?" He held me at arm's length now. "Why I haven't seen such good-doing since . . . since your mother," he said.

"Really? Mom was . . ."

My dad nodded. "A help-the-hapless, save-the-whales, change-the-world do-gooder."

"I didn't know that. I thought she was into like hip-hugger bell-bottoms and disco dancing."

"That, too," my father said. "And any boy who doesn't see how beautiful, bright, and good you are must be blind."

"Thanks, Daddy," I said gratefully.

"You're marking all September third phone calls, right?"

"Absolutely," I said, and sat back down and started highlighting again. I knew Daddy was prejudiced, but I wanted to live up to his expectations. I decided that I needed a complete makeover. But this time I'd make over my soul.

Chapter 18

It was hard not to zone out in Miss Geist's class the day she showed the film clip on natural disasters, but I worked on staying awake. And when my mind did drift, at least I didn't stay totally fixated on why Amber had let a sheep farmer trim her hair.

I had better things to think about. Like I realized I already knew a lot of great souls— like all my friends, in different ways. For example, Christian would drag me to museums all the time. He'd gesture wildly trying to get me to see what he saw in the paintings. It meant a lot to him. In a hideously styleless world, Christian wanted to make things interesting and visual.

Even Murray and Dionne, tangled up in each

145

other as they were, at least knew the value of considering the needs of others.

And poor Miss Geist, who was desperately trying to get us involved no matter how much we resisted.

"Imagine," she said, turning on the lights at the end of the clip, "every single possession, every picture, every memory, everything you worked your whole life for, gone in a second. Can anyone tell us what that might feel like?"

Elton raised his hand.

Miss Geist raised her eyebrows. "Elton?" she said, surprised.

"Can I use the pass?" he asked.

She nodded. "So for the Pismo Beach Disaster Relief effort, we'll be collecting blankets, disposable diapers, and canned food. Who'd like to volunteer?"

It was so weird raising my hand. I was almost embarrassed. Miss Geist was kind of shocked, too. "Cher?"

Everyone turned to look at me. There was some snickering from the back rows. I cleared my throat. Finally, I said, "I want to help."

"Daddy!" I hollered. "You didn't like that vichyssoise, did you?"

I tossed the soup cans into the Gucci suitcase sitting on the counter. I was in the kitchen that night, packing food for the Pismo Beach Disaster Relief Committee. I'd pulled everything we could spare out of the cabinets. Next to the suitcase was a pyramid of cans containing oysters, cherries in brandy, and other gourmet treats.

Daddy, Josh, Logan, and some other guys had taken over the dining room table. It was covered with legal pads, depositions, books, briefs, and folders. I walked past them, lugging the suitcase and two garbage bags full of food to the front door.

Josh and my dad looked up, looked at each other, and shook their heads.

Upstairs, I rotated my closet rack, looking for warm outfits to donate. I thought if I'd been flooded out of my home, I'd love terry lounging pajamas and a contrasting silk kimono top. And shorts or miniskirts, lots of bright, happy-colored short stuff for wading through the ruins. I got all the clothes together and then checked the storage closet, which was bursting with perfect relief items: blankets, an old sleeping bag, a tennis racquet no one ever used anymore, even a pair of skis!

I was struggling with the stuff. The clothes, blankets, and sleeping bag I could just sort of push or drag to the door. But I had to carry the skis, tennis racquet, and some of the outfits, which were still in cleaning bags.

Daddy looked up as I was passing the dining room. "What is it that you're doing?"

"I'm a field captain for Pismo Beach Disaster Relief," I explained.

"I don't think they'll need your skis," he said.

"Daddy, some people lost all their belongings! Don't you think that includes athletic equipment?" I walked on, but not before I saw Daddy glower at Josh and say, "This is your doing, isn't it?"

"As if!" I called over my shoulder.

There were tables set up at one end of the cafeteria in front of this major Pismo Beach Disaster Relief wall banner. Tai and I had been avoiding each other since our blowout. But I got Dionne, Elton, and Amber to join the relief effort. We were all sitting behind different collection tables. Mine was for canned goods donations.

A sign of how much I'd changed, I think, was the fact that I had this big really unattractive label with the word *Captain* on it stuck to one of my best jackets. I didn't even mind that the label was white with red trim and here I was in yellow plaid.

A kid from my history class brought a big bag over to my table. I looked through it. "Decent!" I complimented him. "I'll take the cans, and the blanket goes to table four."

Miss Geist walked by. "Excuse me, I need more boxes, Miss Geist. These are filled."

"Already? Great."

"I divided them into entrées and appetizers," I told her.

Her hair was a miracle. I don't know who was styling it. The harsh rat's nest coif had been tamed and excellently reorganized. But she seemed as confused as ever. "Oh . . . okay," she murmured. "I'll have the boxes picked up."

My table was bustling. Travis came by with a carton. I started unloading the cans. Stuck in with them were some surfing posters, skateboard decals, and other weird-looking paraphernalia. One of my new resolutions was to be part of the solution not the problem. So I was way polite. "Proper! Thanks, Travis," I said.

His face lit up. "Oh, I wasn't sure. I don't need them anymore, but far be it from me to deny anyone else."

"Let's see, I think housewares might be the place for these."

"Hey, I been meaning to tell you something," he said. "I'm sorry about your shoes."

"What shoes?"

"The ones I ruined. Red, with strappy things," he said.

"Those shoes are so last season. I've moved on. What made you even think of them?"

"One of my steps is to say 'sorry' a lot. See, I joined this club with a bunch of steps."

"Twelve?" I said. "Like you joined AA?"

Travis's mouth fell open. Like everything else about him, it was loosely hinged. "How'd you know?"

"Wild guess," I said, and laughed.

He joined in, then said, "Oh, here," and handed me a flyer.

"ASL?"

"Amateur Skateboarding League," Travis explained. "The clarity thing's getting me to a whole new level. Would you come Saturday?"

"Sure." Once that invitation would've meant Travis was out of touch with reality. But I'd just accepted it without a second thought. Being a soul in transition was full of surprises.

"Great," he said. I showed him where Dionne was taking housewares donations. He picked up his carton, said, "Okay, Saturday," and left.

I watched him walk over to De's table. She was no more a fan of the stairwell slackers than I'd been, but she gave Travis a big welcoming smile. This do-good stuff was rampantly contagious.

Chapter 19

The skate park was near the ocean. There was a nice breeze coming off the foam. The place was crawling with guys in knee-length cutoffs and tent-size T-shirts. Everyone was wearing someone. If it wasn't Bob Marley, it was Snoop Doggy Dogg, Billy Idol, or Johnny Depp. It looked like T-shirts of the rich and indicted.

The crowd was rambunctious, hooting and cheering even the practice stunts. But if you listened for it, you could actually hear the waves slapping the beach out behind the contest ramps and slides. I was sitting on a blanket near this totally impossible upside-down horseshoe-type jump. I was just wondering whether Travis could handle it, when someone said, "Hi."

I looked up into the sun and kind of shaded

my eyes. Tai was standing there. Her hair was in pigtails. She looked about ten years old. "Uh . . . hi."

"Can I talk to you?" she said.

"Sure, sit down." I moved over, making room for her on the blanket.

"Cher, I've been in total agony all week. I can't believe I went off like I did."

"No, I've been going down a shame spiral," I said quickly. "I can't believe how unsupportive I was of your feelings for Josh."

"You're entitled to your opinions. I was the 'tard, and you've always been super-nice."

"Not even! If it wasn't for me, you never would've liked a loser like Elton—even if he is in turnaround now, collecting blankets for Pismo Beach and all. I'm so sorry."

"No, I'm sorry. Unbelievable," Tai said, "now I'm going to cry."

"Tai, you pronounced it right! You said, 'unbelievable.' Let's never fight again."

We fell into each other's arms, snuffling and hugging and happy. "Oh, Tai, I missed you. Isn't this great?" I said. "If Travis hadn't invited me, this might never have happened."

"I know," Tai said shyly. "That's why I asked him to."

Travis's name was announced over the loud-speaker. "Look, there he is! Number fourteen," I said.

"He waved to us!" Tai shouted.

"He waved to *you*," I corrected her.

Travis warmed up for a minute, then jumped his board onto the horseshoe-shaped ramp and started doing these brutally mind-boggling moves. He was practically horizontal when he flipped his board in the air. Tai and I went berserk cheering. Travis, completely serious and intense, sailed up and down the sides of the ramp, executing this totally amazing series of skateboard stunts. He was awesome. He was excellent.

"I had no idea he was so motivated," I said.

"Oh, I did." Tai smiled, then she squeezed my hand. "I'm pretty good at picking winners. I mean, look at the great friends I've got."

When the scores were announced, Travis raised his board over his head. He was practically glowing with victory. Tai was glowing, too, with pride.

The place was pandemonium after the events. "Let's find him," I said, tugging Tai up.

"He did pretty good," she said as we made our way through the crowd. "I mean coming in sixth when all the other guys are much older."

"Yeah, those guys should be pros already." I couldn't believe how happy I was for Travis. I was so impressed, watching him all full of concentration and excellence. Admiring Travis felt much better than looking down on him.

We spotted him standing in a circle of excited boardees. They were slapping fives and laughing. He saw us and waved us over. There was this little girl with him.

"You were great!" Tai said.

Travis tossed back his floppy center-parted hair and hugged her. "Ay, I'm glad you guys came. Want to go eat something?"

"Sure," Tai said.

"Let me just finish here. This is Jenny. She's like ten years old, right? And she's doing an article for her school paper."

"We'll hang," I said.

"What was it like doing your first contest?" the little girl asked him.

He answered her, and she listened and wrote things down. "It's kind of tough going along with rules, you know," Travis said. "Like when you're in the moment and you feel a heel-flip or a 180, it's like, 'Why do I have to follow a program?'"

"You know what, Cher?" Tai said. "You'll think I'm a royal airhead, but I really like Travis."

"Yeah," I said, "I can see why."

"I wish there was someone you could like."

I thought about it. "I guess some people are supposed to be alone," I said.

"Hey, you know who'd be good for you?"

"Who?"

"Josh," Tai said.

My mouth flopped open. "You mean that?"

"Absolutely. You guys are perfect together."

"Yeah, but Josh can't stand me," I confided.

"You are so wrong."

"Please. He's always making fun of me."

"That's 'cause he likes you."

"Really?" I asked.

"If he didn't like you, he wouldn't bother teasing you."

"You think?"

"Seriously," Tai said. "He's just being shy. Give him time."

I have to say I liked the way Tai's hair looked in pigtails. I braided mine that night, then went into the dining room to help Josh and Daddy's assistant, Logan, work on the depositions.

"You look like Pippi Longstocking," Josh said, pulling out the chair next to his for me. I tried to believe what Tai had said about his teasing me.

He'd gotten a haircut. "You look like Forrest Gump," I told him. Josh laughed, like ha-ha. But when he thought I wasn't looking, I caught him peeking at his reflection in the window and trying to fix his hair.

"Who's Pippi Longstocking?" I asked.

"Someone Mel Gibson never played."

"How droll."

He got busy with the papers, and I pulled the rubber bands out of my hair and undid the braids. A couple of minutes later, I finished marking the deposition I was working on and reached over to take a new one off the stack. My arm accidentally brushed Josh's. He glanced at me and smiled. He was about to say something when Logan went postal.

"What happened to the August twenty-eighth files?" He was all quivering and panicked.

"What?" Josh asked.

"Mel wanted them tonight. There were twice as many!"

I looked down quickly to check my depos. I had a bad feeling about this.

"He's going to go ballistic!" Logan said. "Where are they?"

"I . . . uh . . . think I checked them for September third conversations."

"What!?" Josh and Logan yelled together.

"Where did you put them?" Josh asked.

"They're divided into the other piles? Is that wrong?"

Logan lost it. "I can't believe it! I've got to redo all that." He turned on me. "What are you, some kind of idiot?"

"Hey," Josh said. "Take it easy. She didn't know."

"She just set us back a day! Who cares about the September call, now we're dead."

"I'm sorry," I said.

Logan grabbed the file out of my hand. "Just forget it, go back to the mall or something."

I'd tried to help, and now I'd ruined things for Daddy.

"What's your problem?" Josh was saying to Logan. "She didn't mean any harm."

I pushed back my chair and ran out of the room.

"I'm going to get killed because she's a moron," I could hear Logan holler.

"She's not a moron, and if you were paying

attention to your assignment, this wouldn't have happened."

I got to the entranceway. I felt too sick to run upstairs to my room, so I just sat down on the bottom step and hid my face in my hands.

Logan charged out of the dining room. "If you weren't busy playing footsie with the dumb kid, she wouldn't be bothering."

Josh was hot on his heels. "What are you talking about?" he demanded.

"You know what I'm talking about. This is a multimillion-dollar suit, not some excuse for puppy love."

"We've been working our butts off on this case," Josh protested.

"Thanks. Keep it up and soon we'll be back to square one." Logan stormed past me into Daddy's office. Josh turned around and saw me sitting there. He was shocked.

"Did I really ruin Daddy's lawsuit?" I asked him.

He sat down next to me. "No, of course not."

"Will he be set back? There's so much work to be done. He can't afford to lose any time."

"Don't worry, I can straighten it out. Your father won't lose any time."

"Poor Daddy."

Josh shook his head. "Boy, where does Logan come off worrying you like this. He screwed up by not watching, and then he tried to blame it on me. Imagine saying we were . . . you know . . . I mean, you're Mel's daughter."

"And you're like a son to him." It was the first time I'd admitted this to Josh or even to myself.

He was pleased. There was this little grin creeping across his face. He tilted his head and looked at me. "But it's not as if we were brother and sister," he said.

"No," I agreed.

"We were just helping."

"That's right," I said, trying to be all indignant. "You've been very dedicated to this case."

"Well, it's a good learning experience, at least for me. I want to be a lawyer, but you, you don't have to do this. You could be having fun, going shopping."

I couldn't believe it. Now Josh was turning on me, too. "You think that's all I do, right? I'm a superficial ditz brain with a credit card."

"No, no, no. I didn't mean that, Cher. I just think, you know, this is how nerds spend their time. You're young and beautiful and . . ."

Beautiful? He thought I was beautiful? "And . . ." I said hopefully.

Josh was as wigged by his blurting as I was. "Uh . . . and what?" he said cautiously.

"You think I'm beautiful?"

He looked away, then back. "Come on, you know you're gorgeous and popular and all. But that's not why I'm here. It's a good learning experience for me."

"You said that already," I pointed out.

"And I want to help your father. Mel's like the only one who cares about me."

I started to say something, then stopped and thought about it. Finally, I kind of whispered, "No, he's not."

We stared at each other silently for a moment. I couldn't believe I'd just admitted that I cared about Josh. Josh, I could tell, wasn't even sure he'd heard right.

"He's not?" he said.

What if he thought I was crazy? What if he hated me and here I was like telling him the truth. What if he turned me down?

"Uh . . . no," I said.

"Are you saying you care about me?"

"I'm just saying . . . I mean, you know, I . . ." I couldn't say it again. I couldn't believe he was *making* me say it again. Before I knew what was happening, I was hitting his arm, going, *"Joossh."*

He grabbed my hand to stop me. Then he lifted up my face and leaned over . . . and kissed me. His lips were much softer and warmer than they looked. They were perfect. I could have kept mine pressed against them forever. When we broke, we sort of stared at each other, still in shock. It was like, what was that? Was it okay? Did it really happen? Then we both started smiling, because it was okay. It was so okay, actually, that we decided to try it again.

Well, you can guess what happened next. . . .

Chapter 20

The bridal gown was totally traditional. It was all acres of creamy antique lace trimmed with teeny white pearls. Our backyard, where the wedding was taking place, was beyond beautiful. Lucy had spoken to the gardener. Not only had José trimmed and planted and cleaned and buffed, but he'd made these towering arrangements of fruit and flowers for the buffet tables. Christian had seen them in a back issue of *Town and Country* and worked on them with José.

Miss Geist was a totally brilliant bride.

Hello, who did you think I was talking about? I mean, I'm only sixteen, and this is California, not Kentucky.

Dionne and Summer were fussing with Miss Geist's train, while I held her bouquet. Our bridesmaid dresses were pale pink and rampantly slinky. When the music began, Miss Geist took off her glasses and gave us all a big hug. Then we took our places for the march down the aisle.

The groom was waiting with the minister in the shade of an ivy-covered bower, also Christian's idea. Mr. Hall was totally resplendent. His dove gray top hat was stylish and distinguished, and excellently hid his baldness.

The music played. Dionne and I started down the aisle, sneaking waves to our friends. Tai winked at us. She and Travis were sitting together, all dressed up and starry-eyed. Elton waved. He was in a dark suit with matching headphones. Someone must have told Amber that black was back, because she was bandaged in it head to toe. Her one deviation from somber was a huge feathery black hat. She looked like the head of an orphanage. And she'd managed to scrunch herself in next to Josh. Who hardly noticed her, of course. Because he couldn't take his eyes off me.

I blew him a kiss, and then the gasps and oohs and aahs began. Miss Geist was coming down the aisle. Dionne burst into tears. Murray, who was sitting on the other side of Josh, got all embarrassed and shook his head at her. But I was getting misty-eyed, too. Especially, when the minister started asking Miss Geist and Mr. Hall did they and would they and other wedding stuff like did anyone mind.

After the ceremony, we were all talking about

the kind of weddings we'd like and what we'd want to wear. We were sitting at one of the big round tables set up under the trees. Amber strolled over. "Well, I for one, am so glad I wasn't asked to be a bridesmaid," she said. "My skin cannot take synthetics."

"Amber, your daddy's rich," De told her. "Why doesn't he buy you a clue?"

"Well, I'm just saying what I think."

"Then don't think so much," Tai advised her.

"Girls," Ms. Stoeger bellowed. "She's going to throw the bouquet."

We all popped up to go. Josh took my arm. "We've got a pool to see whose girl gets the bouquet. It's up to two hundred dollars," he said.

I laughed and squeezed his hand. "It's in the bag."

We assembled on the lawn near Christian's favorite piece of sculpture. Miss Geist tossed the bouquet over her shoulder. She might as well have fired a gun in the middle of a buffalo herd. Suddenly everyone started shrieking, running, jumping, shoving, and pushing to get the flowers. We all landed in a heap on the ground. It was a total fashion pileup. I was buried under a ton of summery pastels. Oh, yes, and one dark ensemble, which was shedding feathers like a flock of deranged birds.

Finally, the heap separated. One girl after another got up. I was the last to emerge, torn, disheveled, blowing feathers off my face, but victorious. I held up the bouquet so that Josh could see it. He gave me a million-dollar smile.

Then a hand clamped down on Josh's shoulder, and there was Daddy. He had a familiar grin on his face as he walked Josh over to me.

"You won the case, didn't you?" I said, giving him a big hug.

"Of course," he said. "You and Josh did a great job helping out. Who's that woman over there?" he asked suddenly. "The big one squeezed into the flowered dress that looks just like one of yours?"

"Uh . . . that's Lucy, Daddy. You know Lucy. She's our maid."

"Really?" He scrunched up his eyes and stared hard at her. "I thought she looked familiar."

"Thank you for all this, Daddy. Everyone's having such a great time," I said.

The three of us stood there silently for a minute, staring out at the party. It was an impressive panorama. There were tons of wedding guests, piles of fabulous food, and a dance floor set up over the swimming pool. Elton and Amber were heading toward it. Dionne and Murray were talking with the newlyweds. Tai and Travis were sitting on the grass, under a tree. By his hand motions I could see he was explaining some complicated stunt to her. Tai was spellbound.

"Thanks for what? You did this," my father said. "You see that bride and groom who can't take their eyes off each other? You did that, Cher. You're the most beautiful girl here—inside and out." He picked one of Amber's feathers out of my hair. "I only wish your mom was here. She'd be so proud of you."

"Really?" I asked.

"Totally," he said.

CHER'S GUIDE FOR THE CHRONICALLY CLUELESS

JUST FOLLOW THIS SIMPLE GLOSSARY, AND A WORLD OF CHILLING BALDWINS AND BETTYS WILL OPEN BEFORE YOU

and • I'm • all (and im ol), 1. I was saying things such as. *He's all "where were you?" and I'm all "what's it your business" and he's all.*

as • if! (az if), exclamation. 1. to the contrary. 2. no way.

Au • di (aw de), 1. goodbye, I'm leaving. 2. I'm out of here. *I'm Audi.*

Bald • win (bawld win), n. 1. attractive guy. 2. a male Betty.

Bar • ney (bar ne), n. 1. unattractive guy. 2. not a Baldwin.

Bet • ty (be te), n. 1. a beautiful woman. 2. a female babe.

big • time (big tim), 1. totally. 2. very.

bug • gin' (bug un), v. 1. irritated, perturbed. 2. flipping out. *I'm buggin'.*

chro•nic (kron ik), adj. 1. dynomite.

clue•less (kloo les) 1. lost, stupid. 2. mental state of people who aren't your friends; uncool.

do•able (du abel) 1. romantically attractive. 2. has mate potential.

dope (dop), adj. 1. smart, cool, especially an idea.

furiously (fur e us le), adj. 1. very, extremely. 2. majorly.

gol•den (gol din), adj. 1. righteous, special.

hot•tie (ho te), n. 1. a gorgeous girl. 2. a babe.

hang (ha ng), v. 1. get tight with. 2. ally with.

hurl (he rl), v. 1. barf, worship the porcelain god. 2. spew, blow chunks.

Jeep•in' (je pin), v. 1. socializing in a Jeep.

loqued out (loked out), 1. souped up. 2 tricked out.

ma•jor•ly (ma jor le), 1. very. 2. totally, furiously.

men•tally chal•lenged (menta le chaleng d), adj. 1. stupid. 2. clueless.

mon•ster (mon ster) 1. much too big and loud. 2. very good. *Monster sound system.*

Mon•et (mo nay), 1. looks fine from a distance, but really a mess up close. 2. not a babe, really.

po•stal (po stal), adv. 1. a state of irrational psychotic anger and disorientation. 2. whacko, flipped.

ran•dom (ran dum), adj. 1. mediocre. 2. whack (sort of).

snag (snag), v. 1. pick up, appropriate, steal. 2. cop.

tard (tar d) (English from retard), n. 1. insensitive, stupid, or childish person.

t.b. (tee bee), 1. true blue. 2. loyal, faithful. 3. totally.

tscha! exclamation. 1. surely you jest.

tow up (toe up), 1. torn up, in bad condition. 2. trashed, toast.

toast (toe st), 1. in trouble, doomed, exhausted. 2. towed up, history. *I'm toast.*

wass•up? (see **zup**.)

whack (whack), adj. 1. very negative

what•ev•er! (wat EV er), exclamation. 1. don't bug me! 2. let's not argue; whatever you say.

wig (wig), v., **wiggin'** or **wigged**. 1. become irrational, freak out. 2. go postal.

wo•man (wu man), n. 1. your boyfriend's name for you.

zup? (zup), question. 1. is anything new? 2. what's up?

About the Author

H. B. Gilmour is the author of *Clarissa Explains It All: Boys, Ask Me if I Care*, the novelization *Pretty in Pink*, and more than fifteen other books for adults and young people.